Heaven

L. L. Fine

Edited by Shannon Cook
Proofread by Julie Phelps

TO MY CHILDREN

TABLE OF CONTENTS

ACKNOWLEDGMENTS   VII
DEATH IS WHEN IT ALL BEGINS   1
AWAKENING   3
MEMORY 1   6
BODY   7
RULES   14
SENSES   19
MEMORY 2   28
THE PUB   29
THE CITY   41
SABERTOOTH   51
MEMORY 3   58
DEATH   60
ESCAPE   67
GLIMPSE   73
MEMORY 4   76
RAINBOW   77
A ROOM   82
MEMORY 5   85
INSIGHT   89
MEMORY 6   94
EXIT   98
MEMORY 7   101
MONSTER   105
MEMORY 8   109
LEPRECHAUN   114
MEMORY 9   117
EASTER EGG   120
MEMORY 10   123
TREE   125
BATTLE   129
PRISON   136
MEMORY 11   143

SHATTERING   144
CORE   151
CONTACT   157
VISIT   163
DEPORTATION   171
DECISION   177
FROM THE AUTHOR   181
ABOUT THE AUTHOR   183

ACKNOWLEDGMENTS

First of all: this is **not** a book about Google. It's not connected to Google in any way, and implies nothing about this company (which I really like, by the way). It's a work of fiction, taking place in the not so distant future. Any resemblance of names, locations, trademarks, etc. mentioned in this book, to real names, trademarks etc. is strictly coincidental. All the events, names and places described here are completely fictitious.

Having stated that, I'd like to thank my editor, Shannon Cook, for her wise advice, great knowledge and skills; my wife, for without her none of this could have happened; and my kids – for giving me hope that tomorrow will come.

DEATH IS WHEN IT ALL BEGINS

AWAKENING

My first day in Heaven was hell.

It started just the way you always hear: with a white light, very bright. But there was no choir of angels and I did not feel peace. On the contrary. Between my ears a blaring horn went off, accompanied by a splitting headache. Actually, it was more than just a headache—it was a body ache. The kind that cuts through you from every direction, splitting you apart with countless sharp knives, from the inside out. The kind that doesn't even allow you to scream. A grenade blowing up inside of you.

You know how it is when a child is injured? How at first there are no sounds coming out of his mouth? Even though it was a hard blow and he is obviously in pain, his eyes open wide and his mouth opens in a silent scream, and the more time that passes, the more obvious it is that the pain is getting stronger?

That's exactly how it was.

But I was not a child. When I finally tried to push air through my lungs, to let out the massive pain, there was no air there; in fact, there were no lungs. There was only eternal emptiness, endless pain, and a white light penetrating through every pore, searing my soul. I did the only thing I could do.

*

-*"What was that?"*
-*"I blacked out."*

*

When I woke again, everything was calmer. The white light was still there, washing over everything, but every now and then I could see signs of gray around it. The horn turned into an annoying but tolerable buzz. The pain was still there, but it was no longer the pain of a cut, but of healing. It even allowed other sensations to exist beside it. For example, I could feel myself breathing. There was a taste in my mouth. Not a good taste, but a taste.

I heard a voice next to me, but I couldn't understand the language. It was rather pleasant, yes, but I was annoyed that I couldn't understand a word of it. I tried to remember -

But I couldn't remember anything.

My past was white. My identity was a buzz. My present was pain.

I closed my eyes and the white light went out.

*

"Good morning." I heard the voice again.

I understood it!

I understood it.

I opened my eyes. The white light was still there, but it was no longer blinding. More like a general glow which shrouded the details. It was coming from the walls, emanating from the ceiling—there were no lamps on the ceiling, I pointed out to myself—and it created an angelic aura around the woman who had said good morning to me.

She, too, was very pale. She was also quite beautiful and mostly naked. Only three little pasties with a red cross painted on them made her 'mostly' naked. At first I thought they were tattoos—my vision was still blurry, so I didn't really notice where the white pasties ended and where the pale skin began. Only later did I discover this was her take on clothes.

And only later did I find out that she placed those on her body in order to look modest.

*

-"Really?"

-"Yes. But at that moment I just stared at her, fascinated. Over the general white background, she moved like a live, flowing, marble statue with eyes of deep indigo, a mouth the color of cherries, and three red and white pasties."

-"Just the way you like it."

-"Yes. She was also tall and well built. Not an ounce of fat, with hints of swimmers' muscles, long and flowing. She came closer to me with a smile."

*

"Do you feel better?"

She leaned over me with a worried look. I was flooded by the rich aroma coming off of her, and for a moment I lost my focus. Her voice was exceptional, a harmony of different tones, warm and relaxing. She held a flowered teapot that gave off a wonderful smell, too. But who thought of tea at such a time?

I tried to tell her I was feeling better than before, but no sound came out of my mouth. Only smothered screeches of air.

"Don't exhaust yourself. It will come back to you in time. Here, drink."

She poured the tea directly into what should have been my mouth. It was hot and tasted good.

I blinked at her with gratitude.

"This will help you. Go to sleep now."

She put a warm and tender hand on my eyes and I faded to black.

MEMORY 1

It was not total rest.

It was constantly being interrupted. Rips of thoughts. Fragments of memories. Unclear images. Like a nightmare-filled sleep, when you don't really feel awake—but you know the reality around you is not fake. But there were some clear things.

The mist came, the mist went away. I remembered a beautiful woman with warm eyes and brown hair. She looked at me closely, her eyes taking me in joyfully. All of a sudden I felt better. Calmer. I giggled. It was a baby's giggle. I reached a hand to her and the hand was that of a baby as well. Was I a baby? The hand touched her lips; she parted her lips and let my hand in. A flow of new sensations took me over. Warmth. Moist. Wonder. Joy. Lots and lots of joy.

I heard a baby's giggle. It was very close to me. Where? I looked around but didn't find it. Perhaps behind me? No. The baby giggled again. I giggled again. I was the baby and the baby was me. The pretty lady made funny faces at me and laughed and laughed and laughed. "Mommy," I thought. She was Mommy.

A man joined Mommy. A large man with thick brows and a crooked nose. "Daddy," came the thought. He looked at me as well and smiled. But he made me sad. Cold. He said something to the woman and she looked at him and they exchanged words. I didn't understand the words, but I knew they were talking to me. The man reached over and stroked my head. It was pleasant too, but still had an overtone of sadness. I knew he wouldn't be there with me later on. It was Daddy. And Daddy wasn't there. There was a feeling like something bad was about to happen.

The mist came, the mist went away.

BODY

When I regained consciousness, I felt better. The pain had turned into the sensation you feel after a good workout. The noise had turned into a gentle breeze in my ears. The whiteness no longer hurt my eyes. It was just white, clean, and pure.

For the first time in Heaven, I felt like I was in Heaven.

Of course I didn't know it at the time. In fact, I was pretty sure I had survived some horrible accident and was recovering in the hospital. Not that I ever knew of any hospital that looked like that, or a nurse that looked like -

I couldn't remember her name. And I couldn't see her from where I was.

I tried to pull myself up and look around, but soon discovered I couldn't really do that. Not because I was tied up or paralyzed. But because I had no body. No legs, no arms, no stomach—nothing. Instead, where all those were supposed to be, I only sensed that white, blinding light.

If there had been blood in my body, it would undoubtedly have frozen at that moment. I panicked, I am not ashamed to say. I was horrified. A million scenarios went running through my head and none of them were good. Perhaps I was dreaming? Hallucinating? Perhaps I had been abducted, or the accident had been worse than I thought -

The accident. Yes. It was the most likely option. I must have been in an accident. I didn't remember it. I didn't remember anything I had done before I woke up, but I must have been in an accident. I was lying in the hospital and imagining I didn't have -

"I see you noticed you're missing something." I heard a harmonious voice right next to me.

I turned around and looked at her. "What happened to me?" My voice was weak.

"You'll understand it all later on. In the meantime, let's go get you a body."

*

-"How exactly did you move?"

-"She was the one walking. I was somehow in her hands. The white view didn't change much. From my white room we went into a white corridor, but not before she looked around the corner carefully. I didn't know why at the time. After a few quick steps, very fast ones, we arrived at a grand door; hidden behind it was the body warehouse."

-"The what?"

*

It was not exactly a shed. Behind the door was a massive space, endless. Unlike the perfect white of the room I had woken up in, the storage room was completely black. In it floated bodies of people of all sizes, colors, and shapes. Women, men, giants, little people, skinny, old, muscular… every kind you could think of. Hundreds of thousands of bodies. Millions of bodies. Set out on display, rolling slowly, each one entirely illuminated with no visible light source.

I couldn't look away.

"I forgot how impressive this can be when you see it for the first time," she said from my right. I looked at her; she was pale and amazing against the endless, black background. Complete contradiction—spectacular.

I looked to see what we were standing on. It was a floating terrace, very small, like you see on old houses in Italy. Only an ancient, wrought iron rail prevented her from falling into infinity. I didn't have a body, so I couldn't fall… only float in the ocean of motionless people.

"What is it, this place?"

"This is where you pick your body. You need to have one. Which one do you want?"

I looked at her body. That's the one I want, I thought to myself.

"We can arrange this kind of body for you." Her hand slid down her abdomen. "But I think you want it to be on me, not on you. You were a man, right?"

"I was?"

I didn't understand what she was talking about. I didn't like how she was talking. Why did she refer to me in the past tense? I thought she was just confused. Because I was just lying in a hospital somewhere, unconscious. I would wake up soon and everything would be fine.

8

"You were," she repeated. "When you were alive. You were a man. Or were you a lesbian? Because judging by the way you look at me..."

"I was a man. I am a man. What do you mean - when I was alive?"

"You'll understand everything in time. So, a man's body, then, yes?"

"Yes."

"Because you can have a woman's, you kn -"

"A man!"

She smiled and the world changed. A mighty vortex spun the millions of bodies around us and after a few seconds, when everything stabilized, there were only men around us.

"How tall?"

I started to respond, but then I stopped. I didn't know how tall I was. After the initial shock of the body warehouse had passed, the frustration returned. I didn't know anything about myself. And in any case, my thoughts kept going back to this whole 'when you were alive' thing. What was she talking about – 'was'?

She cut into my train of thought. "How tall do you want to be?"

"I don't know!" I said angrily. "Give me a minute!"

"Okay, okay..." She leaned back and tried to hide an impatient expression, after which she stretched like a giant cat coming out of a pool of cream. She looked amazing.

"So... I can just pick my height?"

"Here you can pick everything. Height, weight, eye color. Look around."

*

I needed quite a bit of time. The warehouse had no end or horizon. Only more and more endless, deep darkness filled with human bodies. I could see with no limits. Then I started to notice the details.

Something in the details was wrong.

All the men around me were perfect. A male version of her, if you will. Flawless, physically. Hunks. Muscular, proportional, handsome. They were organized in space in an intricate, multi-dimensional matrix, by color and shape with multi-dimensional logic. It took one look around to understand that if the veranda floated in a different direction, there would be Nordic men, blond - and in another

9

direction they would be Africans. More yellowish, Asian skin colors would be in a different direction, and going further in would allow you to browse different body types. But not every type was there.

"Why are there no fat men here?"

"There are," she answered. And the world spun around again.

I was surprised. I expected our balcony to fly in one of the directions, but the opposite happened. We stayed in place and the men's matrix matched itself to us. It was very confusing. In the end, I found myself surrounded by countless fat men.

Some were just a little overweight. Some were very fat and some were morbidly obese. Really big, 'turn-of-the-century Sumo wrestler' types. Mountains of fat everywhere, on the legs, stomach, places where thinner people have necks. Carefully, I tried to navigate myself through the matrix. It wasn't complicated; I just thought of a certain direction and the world spun toward it. Suddenly I feared the white angel would resent my initiative, but she smiled. It seemed like she was happy I was being independent.

One body, floating rather close to me, drew my attention. It wasn't huge, but was certainly heavier than average. A young man with curly brown hair, regular features, kind of short and flaccid looking. He reminded me of something, but I didn't know what it was.

"Do you like it?"

She looked curiously at me. The difference between her perfection and his wretchedness cried up to Heaven. Even if I had wanted him, I wouldn't have picked him. I couldn't bring myself to make her look at me in his neglected form.

"No," I finally said. "Can we go back to the attractive, well-built men?"

"You're the boss," she said with half a smile. The men swirled in front of my eyes again and I started to dig deeper. Choosing my body seemed very tiring all of a sudden. How can you pick from endless possibilities? What were the criteria for making my choice? What did I even want? And more importantly, why did I want what I wanted?

"How tall are you?" I asked.

"Six feet four," she said.

*

-"When we left the room, I was black."

-"African?"

-"No, no. I mean completely dark. Like the night. Like coal. Just as she was completely white, I was completely black, from head to toe. With dark hands, shiny, smooth black hair, and black lips."

-"Somewhat symbolic."

-"Yes, but I didn't know it at the time."

-"Are you sure?"

- "No, but my eyes were blue as sapphire. Slightly brighter than her indigo."

*

I was six feet five and I had muscles like Superman. I wore a tight robe, black and shiny. It made everything I wanted to hide disappear, but hinted, without a shadow of a doubt, that there was much to conceal.

I was overly excited, I know. But can you blame me? For the first time in my life, I looked the way I wanted to look, the way I deserved to look, and I felt good about it.

So we walked down the hall, black and white, barefoot and clean, at a steady pace, like two noble chess pieces. I breathed Heaven's air for the first time through real lungs. I felt it on real skin. I heard it through real ears.

And I felt good about that, too.

She walked rather quickly, but I insisted on keeping a slower pace. I had a lot to process and the corridor seemed like a good chance to think.

First of all, I tried to figure out what went on there, in the warehouse. Entering the body I picked had been strangely easy. The moment I wanted it, it came to our balcony, right in front of us. I looked at the body closely before I chose. Turned it around in all directions, flipped it over, checked many facial expressions—artificial, but reasonable—lifted his hands up, parted his legs. Then I started toying with the little details. The hairstyle, hair color. The length of the hair. I chose bold in the end. And the eyes: black, white, red, green. I picked what I wanted and then I changed it again. I made the nose wider. I made the nose narrower. And I enhanced the pecs. Then I enhanced them again, then again. When I heard a little giggle from my right, I changed them back.

The moment I picked it, really chose it, I just went in it. It's a bit

11

hard to explain. I was floating forward and I entered it. One fuzzy moment—and I looked out of his eyes, over to the balcony. She was there, alone, amused. I skipped over the rail and that was all that was needed. I was him and he was me.

It took me a few seconds to get used to myself. First of all, it was clear to me that I had never been six feet five. My body looked at the world from a higher point of view than felt normal. And, of course, I could look at her from above. A refreshing change I easily grew accustomed to.

And the strength I possessed. And the fitness. My stride was light, bouncy. I felt like a tiger. Inhuman. The control over the body was inhuman as well. At first it felt like exoskeleton control—then I tried to remember what exoskeleton meant. I couldn't remember.

*

- *"How did it feel, really, when you couldn't remember?"*
- *"Hard to explain. There were some things that looked natural and some things that looked artificial to me. I couldn't explain why, even to myself.*
"Like having an artificial hand."
"Maybe. I wouldn't know."

*

"Now, perhaps you can tell me what is going on?"
"Not here. Inside the room. "
The way back to my room was much longer than I remembered. I looked around. The corridors were long and completely white. There were no exit signs anywhere. There were no signs at all. But there were people in them. Beautiful people. Fabulous. Women and men in all colors, shapes, and sizes, and all were beautiful. They all looked like they had just come from the body warehouse. Some walked fast like we did. But most looked at themselves while they walked, closing their hands with an observing gaze, patting their tummy, bouncing a little in place. Getting used to their new skin.

Everyone was by themselves, I pointed out to myself. Only we walked together. Eventually we got back to the room that we had started from. The door closed behind us.

"Well, so?"
"Shut up," she said, clinging to me with a kiss.

12

All at once, the world turned red, and flames of pleasure burned me from every side.

RULES

"I'm in heaven."

"Thank you."

I looked at her. I knew nothing about her, but in the past few hours she had made me feel like I knew everything about her. She lay on her back next to me and her eyes were smiling, her lips were inviting, and her hands were a divine wonder I could not stop looking at. She was perfect. Everything was perfect. I couldn't remember who I was, I didn't remember what had happened to me or how I had gotten here. But I did remember there was only one perfect place in the world.

"I mean, I really am in Heaven, aren't I?"

"That's true," she answered after thinking for a moment. With one, flowing motion, she raised herself up to a seated position and the whole bed moved under her. Her hand stroked my thigh. "Was it good for you?"

I was addicted to her touch. I don't think the word 'good' was worthy of describing what I felt. It was not good. It was... divine. It was the best sensation I have ever felt. If I had known that was how Heaven felt, I would probably have arrived here sooner.

"It was okay," I replied.

Her hand paused. "Just okay?"

She sounded disappointed.

"The truth is, I don't know what to compare it to. I can't remember anything before... here," I said and gestured around the room. Next to the bed was the black shiny robe that had been tossed aside. I couldn't remember how it had been removed from my body. Then I remembered how and smiled. Next to her, a little further, three red pasties sparkled. I wondered what the pale woman would do with them later.

"You really don't remember?" she asked.

"No. Nothing."

"But you must remember what your name is. Right?"

"No."

"Hmm." She pulled her knees to her chest and stayed silent for a few seconds. "It happens, every now and then. That people don't remember. I've heard of cases like this. It has something to do with the shock of crossing over. Usually the memories come back rather quickly. Once you choose a body, it shouldn't be a problem anymore. All the memories should be in it, before you even enter." Her facial expression was one of reflection.

"So what does it mean for me?" I questioned carefully.

"I don't know for sure, yet. I've never seen anything like it."

"And who are you, anyway? Why are you here?"

A beaming smile shined on her face.

"I work here. I escort the newcomers."

"Work? In Heaven?"

"It's not Heaven for everyone," she sighed.

"What does that mean?"

"Nothing. I'm just complaining, really." She took my hand in hers and started playing with my fingers, examining them, their strength and flexibility. She entwined them with her fingers and I had trouble concentrating on what she was saying. "There's work everywhere. Even in Heaven. At least for me."

"So you..." I pulled my fingers away from hers eventually, trying to remember the Bible. Surprisingly, I managed to do that easily. "...are some sort of angel?"

Yes, I decided. She had to be an angel. She sure looked like one. Her touch was angelic; when I looked at her my heart skipped a beat. She made me feel as only an angel could make me feel. I could have sworn she was an angel. And if so, then wow, those religious guys had been so wrong all these years....

But her smile only broadened and she let out a jingling laugh.

"Of course not, silly. There are no angels in Heaven. I'm just like you, I came up here from downstairs. I've just been here a little longer. A veteran," she supplied. "And because I understand this place better than most, my job is to welcome them here. You know, soften the blow to new ones, like you."

This was very interesting. I sat up and crossed my legs. "What are they, exactly, new ones?"

"Those who've just come up to Heaven. Those who have no idea what's going on here, what the rules are -"

"Rules?" I interrupted her. "There are rules in Heaven?"

She shrugged. "There are rules everywhere."

I didn't like it. "It sounds too much like..."

I hesitated for a moment. I had meant to say the place where I had lived my previous life, but I didn't know what to call it. I knew I had lived on Earth. But where exactly was Heaven in relation to it? In space? On some spiritual, divine plane? My mind was filling with new questions at a dizzying rate. "What did you say earlier? Downstairs?"

"Yes, that's what we call it. Downstairs." Her indigo eyes shone and stared at me. "And what do you remember from life downstairs?"

I remembered almost nothing. There were vague fragments of pictures, sensations, but I didn't know how much of it was related to me at all, or how real they were. I tried to think about my previous life. I couldn't remember anything tangible. But I knew some general things.

"Rules, punishment, borders... work. That's how it is downstairs, right? And if all that exists even after you go up to Heaven, then what's the difference really?"

She started laughing. At first it was a giggle, then another one, and then many more. Her entire body was shaking. She fell onto her back, tears of laughter in her eyes. I looked at her with renewed amazement. Have I mentioned she was more beautiful than anyone else I had ever seen?

Eventually she managed to speak again. She rose on her elbows and looked at me mischievously. "Now, tell me the truth: Everything you've accepted from me here, in the past few hours, did you ever get that downstairs, when you were alive? Yes, I know you don't remember, but try and guess. Have you been with anyone like me?"

"I don't... well, probably not. Is it like that here all the time?"

"No. You're just starting. It will get better."

"And that's the big difference?"

She shook her head and climbed off the bed. She looked around and located her pasties and walked toward them. I was fascinated by the way her back was straight and her body flowing.

"I can't say it's the biggest difference," she said over her shoulder. "But yes, it's one of them. Understand this: everything here is better. Stronger. More alive." She bent over and reclaimed her pasties. "Unlike you, I remember what I had down there. This is a zeta times better. But do you know what the best thing here is?"

She turned around and sent me a teasing look.

"Well?"

"You cannot die here."

For a brief moment of silence, our eyes locked. Then we both broke out in thundering laughter. Sure, you couldn't die here. Time didn't matter either. And if you cannot die and time doesn't matter, then the rules don't really exist. Neither do borders. And as if to prove the point, she came back to the bed, shamelessly leaning against me. As if she belonged there. I accepted her into my arms with the exact same feeling. Her body was firm, strong, and heavy on me. But my body knew how to handle it well.

"So can we... again?" I asked.

"My pleasure," she said, and began removing those pasties again.

*

-*"Again!"*
-*"Yes. We did it a few more times."*
-*"I thought she was too busy for that."*
-*"Yeah, I thought so too. But no matter what other job she had to do, she wasn't in a rush to do it."*

*

In between those few more times, I learned a few more things. In Heaven, it turns out, you don't really have to do all kinds of trivial things. Like eating or drinking, for example. Visiting the bathroom is not particularly necessary. On the other hand, if you choose to eat or drink, then wow. Like she said: zeta times better. Same with the bathroom, by the way. Or a warm bath.

Everything really did improve with time. Everything but my memory.

"Is something coming back to you?" she asked after a few more hours.

I shook my head. It bothered me greatly.

"Nothing. As if I was born here. I can't remember anything from my life."

Her brows furrowed. "That's not how it should be. Your memory should have returned."

"Some of my memory did come back. I remember how to talk, the language, so -"

She shook her head. "That's not how it works here. No matter what language you spoke downstairs, now you speak something else. Everyone speaks the same language here."

"What language is it?"

"It's just the language. It doesn't matter what you spoke downstairs. Chinese, Arabic, English. You can speak the language you're used to, but when I hear you, it will be in the language I know. So what language did you think you've been speaking?"

I found out, to my surprise, that I didn't know that, either. The word 'English' appeared in my thoughts. I knew what English was, apparently. But I didn't know if I had been speaking English. I could have been speaking any language and she would still have understood me. The answer to my lack of memory, it turned out, did not have anything to do with that. But I had an idea.

"Why don't you check with your… boss? Is he around?"

"He's always around. Do you really want me to go?"

I shrugged. "I just want to know who I am. Trash." I placed my hand on my mouth and looked around, worried. "Are you allowed to swear here? Is it… proper?"

She laughed a little again. "You're such a baby, huh? You can't really swear here. I mean, you can try. But all I'll hear is 'trash.' More 'trash' and more 'trash.' And you're right about the boss. I'll go check."

She got out of bed and left the room. It was so fast and sudden, for a moment I didn't know what to do. Her pasties were still on the floor. I rushed to pick them up (they felt very soft in my hand, like silk) and ran out into the hallway, but then I remembered I wasn't wearing anything either and went back to pick up my robe.

About three seconds passed before I exited the room. She was no longer there.

Nor was the hallway.

For the first time, I was in Heaven.

SENSES

I froze in place.

A rich variety of colors hit me. Mighty blues, fierce reds, lively greens, merry oranges. Everything was so shiny, so vivid, and so different from the white and sterile world I had just left. The suddenness of it was physically painful. I immediately decided to go back through the door and re-enter the world I was more used to. When I turned around, of course, there was no door—only another endless kaleidoscope of bright, exciting colors attacking me from all directions. I had to handle it.

I couldn't. I knelt, then curled up in the fetal position and closed my eyes. It helped a little.

But then I noticed the sound. A soft, melodic, wondrous cacophony of leaves blowing in the wind, birds chirping happily, distant bells, growing grass, crashing waves, whispering winds… and human voices, some talking, and some purring with pleasure for reasons that were not hard to guess.

And that scent.

It was unlike anything you could smell downstairs. It was a combination of everything, of all the things that are good, all at once: the wonderful, clear air of secluded mountaintops, the sensual thickness of fresh incense, the pleasant aroma of weed, the salty promise of ocean waves. All together. In each breath.

And I was indeed breathing. Once, twice, ten times.

Gradually, I was able to open my eyes and look around.

The pale woman was not there. Around me were sparse pine woods, like you find in Europe. Yet the trees were like nothing I had ever seen. Generally in Heaven, things are not exactly the same as downstairs. Sometimes they are, like the pineapples and mangoes that were in front of me, but usually everything is upgraded and updated. Downstairs, there aren't really pineapples like those that grow here; they don't grow on trees down there, either. And not all year round. And not right before your eyes, like they were at that moment, in front of me.

*

-"Pineapples on trees?"
-"Yes."
-"Did you try one?"
-"Of course! I couldn't resist."
-"And how was it?"
-"Exactly how you would expect a pineapple growing in Heaven would be. A sweet jolt running through your body, leaving burns of pleasure on your tongue."
-"I never thought of pineapple quite like that."
-"You've never been to Heaven."

*

While recovering from my little taste, I started examining my surroundings more thoroughly. Not only because I was interested in my surroundings, though. More than that, I wanted to test myself. This gorgeous new body of mine, its capabilities, what Heaven allowed it to do.

Seeing into the distance, for example.

I'm not talking about a distance of a mile or two. I am talking about infinity. At first I didn't understand it; it looked like an optical illusion. But when I focused on the pineapple (yes, again) that was dangling off a tree on the next hill, suddenly the fruit grew and filled my field of vision, as if I could reach up and touch it. And I realized that it was indeed possible. And natural. Suddenly it seemed obvious to me: why wouldn't it be like that? Why should distance limit sight?

I had so many questions. I had to find the pale woman, to give me answers.

I didn't understand where she had disappeared to, or why. After all she had said about helping newcomers and after all she had done for me, it was just unreasonable that she had vanished like that. I assumed she would come back quickly. In any case, I figured she couldn't have gone far. I figured the trees must be in my way. So I climbed one of the trees to see further.

Yes, I climbed. It was easy. Two jumps, a hand on a branch, another jump—and I found myself 164 feet off the ground, looking at the most amazing valley I have ever seen. Emerald trees everywhere, bursting with spots of colors—orange, red, yellow—all different kinds of fruits. Far off in the distance, white mountains climbed up to the sky and I could see the detail of the cabins sprinkled around them. On the other side, the sea glistened, a mighty blue ocean. When I focused on it, I could see people swimming and surfing.

Far above, across the background of the deep sky, deeper than anything imaginable, I noticed a magnificent rainbow. It streamed out of a cluster of pink and white clouds and met the ground at the end of what looked like a great jungle. Flocks of birds flew behind it at varying heights. Butterflies fluttered around the trees.

"Hey." I heard a new voice from below.

I looked between the branches. Far below me were a couple of people wearing leopard suits, orange with yellow specks. They smiled at me and waved their hands. "What are you looking for up there?"

I waved back to them and carefully climbed down. Although my pace was fairly quick, it was still a tall tree. So halfway down I got tired of it and just jumped. It seemed natural to me, but only after I let go of the tree did I understand it was over sixty-five feet to the ground. I panicked, trying to understand what in trash's name was I thinking when I had decided to just jump.

*

-"*And you fell down, sixty-five feet??*"
-"*Yes.*"
-"*And what happened?*"
-"*Gravity in Heaven is similar to the gravity downstairs. Since the velocity you develop during the fall is at the same speed, the landing is just as hard.*"

*

The only difference is the body you have. The body I had, a superman's body, survived the fall exactly like Superman. I didn't even feel pain. Just a little - okay, a lot - of pressure on my muscles and joints.

"Don't tell me, you're new here," said the man of the pair. He had a deep, rich voice, very masculine. Up close, I could see the leopard suit was not a suit at all. He, like his partner, was covered from head to toe with a phenomenal coat of cheetah fur. It was just the way their bodies were made, like mine was the color of coal. Aside from the fur, they were completely human—wearing nothing, though the fur concealed everything necessary.

21

"How did you know I was new?"

He answered with a smile, "I couldn't understand, at first, why you were climbing down so carefully…"

"… But then you jumped," continued the woman, "and we weren't sure…"

"… Until we saw you freak out on the way down," the man finished.

"Welcome to Heaven," they said together, extending their hands.

I shook the man's hand with my right and the woman's hand with my left. Both hands had a warm, furry touch. I had a feeling that if they wanted to, they could extend claws.

"I'm Jackie," said the woman. "My husband's name is José. And you are…?"

Her husband? In Heaven? I remembered what the pale woman had said about rules. Not that I have anything against marriage, but somehow, well, I didn't think it was supposed to be like that in Heaven. On the other hand, I didn't really know that much.

"Hmm… I don't really know," I said hesitantly.

"Oh, so you haven't decided on your new name yet. A lot have doubts at first."

"No, no. I just don't remember it. I arrived here a few… days ago, I think. And since then, I've been trying to remember my name and who I was downstairs, but nothing's coming back to me. I know it's weird, my angel said -"

"Your what?"

"I know, I know, she's not a real angel. I mean the woman who accompanied me. The one who welcomed me here."

The couple exchanged glances.

"I don't really understand what you mean," said José.

And his wife continued, "What do you mean, welcomed you here?"

I looked to where I had found myself when I arrived in the woods. I hoped that at any moment a door would open over there and the pale woman would come out of it and explain everything to them. But, of course, no door opened. I had to manage it on my own. "When I woke up here, in Heaven, there was a woman who took care of me. She helped me at first, took me to where you pick out a body…." Doubt made my voice drop lower, and I asked softly, "I don't understand. You didn't have an escort?"

"No one has an escort," said Jackie.

22

"At least not that we've ever heard of," José added.

"We've been here for… how many years, my sweet?" she asked.

José answered, "Sixty-eight years, honey."

"Sixty-nine, I think. In July," she corrected him.

"You're right, my love. If you knew, why did you ask?"

"I wanted to know that it means as much to you, my dear."

They drew closer for a passionate kiss. Which went on. And on.

*

-*"What a nauseating couple. I hate those."*

-*"Aren't they nauseating? They kept smiling at each other, holding hands and kissing. I started to feel very uncomfortable around them."*

-*"Well, no need to exaggerate."*

-*"Like two teenagers in love, I tell you. In cheetah-colored fur, of all things, and completely naked."*

-*"Did you say anything about it to them?"*

-*"No. I just tried to look the other way."*

*

"Are you sure about what you're saying?" Jackie detached herself from José at last. "Perhaps it has something to do with your memory loss? That too, by the way, is something that's never happened here. When people come up here, they come with all their memories. Otherwise, what's the point?"

"But she said it happens every now and then," I tried to explain.

"Who is this 'she,' anyway? What's her name?"

What was her name?

"She didn't tell me."

Jackie's brows lifted in disbelief. "And you say you've been with her for a few days?"

"I'm not sure anymore. It seemed like days… when I woke up, I was in this white room -"

"Yes, that's what happens when you come up here. And you say she was already there?"

"Yes. No. Maybe. What I'm sure of is that she arrived very quickly, yes."

They exchanged glances again. "It doesn't make any sense." This time, José spoke first. "The awakening room is a private thing. You

23

cannot enter someone else's room."

"But the fact is, she did. Then she took me to this… warehouse of bodies."

"Took you? How?"

"I don't know!" I yelled in frustration. "It seemed like she took me by the hand. I can't explain, I'm new here!"

"Alright, alright. Let's calm ourselves down a little. I'm sure there's a logical explanation for it." Jackie took my hand in hers and stroked it. It was pleasant. Not in the same way as with the pale woman. But still pleasant. "Basically, after the awakening and a short recuperation period, you're supposed to find yourself—alone—in the body warehouse, and then you pick yourself out a body. But it's a private, personal experience. It doesn't exist in the outside world, from what I know." She pointed to José and then herself. "Even us, coming to Heaven together, each of us woke up alone and we only met after we picked a body."

I noted to myself that it was very strange that they had picked the same body type if they woke up separately. And what did it mean that they came up to Heaven together? Did they kill themselves? But those who commit suicide don't go to Heaven… maybe they were just in an accident? The questions popped up in my head, but I didn't want to change the subject. There is a time and a place for everything. Right now, what I cared about most of all was what the trash was happening here. And who the trash I was.

"Okay, so in my case it was different. She took me, took care of me, she even…" I smiled shyly, "… never mind."

They looked at each other knowingly. I continued. "We were together for quite a while. But you say there's no such thing?"

"Exactly. It's impossible."

"Well, I didn't imagine it."

From the look they exchanged, I realized I wasn't being very persuasive.

"So where is she now?" Jackie asked simply.

"I don't know that, either. She went out the door and disappeared. When I tried to follow her, I found myself here. But she was gone. Oh—she said she had to go to her boss and talk to him."

"Her boss?"

"Come on," I pointed up. "God. He's supposed to always be around, right?"

The couple looked like a very hard rock had hit them. They both

24

stood open-mouthed. José looked at me in disbelief. Jackie just sat down abruptly on her butt, trying not to laugh, but a few snorts came out anyway.

I didn't really understand what the joke was.

"Tell me, my friend," José said as he placed a friendly hand on my shoulder, "where exactly do you think you are?"

"In Heaven, right?"

"Yes, but which Heaven, exactly?"

*

-"*You're telling me you didn't know?*"

-"*Exactly. I didn't know at first. And yes, I had many questions, but Jackie and José refused to answer them until we'd had a drink together.*"

-"*What do you mean, drink?*"

-"*Exactly what you think. When they said drink, they actually meant drink. But before that, they taught me how to beam.*"

*

They had not planned on teaching me that. They just asked me to follow them, looked forward, and suddenly turned, one after the other, into two light beams that ended at the top of one of the trees a few hundred feet from me. After a second they beamed over the mountain and disappeared completely.

I stood alone, shocked.

After a moment they beamed back, arguing.

"I told you!" Jackie was furious at José. "He doesn't know how to beam!"

"Alright, alright, my lemon drop. I thought he was just delayed."

"My mature watermelon, he is like a baby that needs to be taught everything. Don't forget."

"Alright, alright, my marshmallow. You are right."

"What the trash just happened here?" I tried to end the argument.

"I was right, that's what happened." Jackie glowed with pride, but didn't even look at me.

"So you were right! Why do you always have to be right?"

"I don't have to, kit-kat. That's just the way it always is."

"Is not! Not always -"

"Don't argue, jelly bean."

"Okay, my ice cream sandwich."

I stood patiently aside, trying not to get a sugar rush. Finally, they both turned their attention back to me. "Is it true you don't know how to beam?" José asked.

"I don't even know what beaming is," I admitted. "I'm new here." It was beginning to sound like a sentence I would be repeating over and over again, until time collapsed into itself and turned into a kangaroo.

"Beaming is like walking really far, but much more useful. You just have to look at the point you want to go to - wait, do you know how to farscope?"

"You mean," I guessed, "when you focus on a far point and see it as if it's close?"

"Yes, good, you know. So you need to farscope where you want to be and then…."

He started making motions with his hands and legs, trying to show me what to do. "Jackie, how do I explain this to him?"

His wife tried to help him "Then you just go there, with your mind. As if you were a laser beam."

José wasn't happy with the explanation. "Not exactly walking," he said. "You have to visualize yourself there."

"Visualizing won't help him, lemon pie. He's like a baby. We need to use terms he knows."

"Here, look." José looked to the right and beamed eighty feet in that direction. "Now you!" he shouted across the distance.

Now me. I didn't really know what I was doing, but I did what seemed natural for me to do. I focused on one point, next to José, until I saw it clearly. Then I tried to imagine myself there.

Nothing happened.

I blinked my eyes, trying to focus harder, to actually visualize myself standing there next to him. Still nothing happened.

"Visualize hard!" he yelled.

It didn't work for me.

"Try imagining you're walking there, taking one giant step," Jackie, standing next to me, offered.

Suddenly she wasn't next to me, she was eighty feet behind me.

"Great!" José rejoiced.

"What are you so happy about? Your orange spouse was right again!"

Actually, I didn't say that to him.

*

-"Sounds amazing, to beam."
-"The truth is that my first beams were not spectacular. Something in my focusing ability was not working and a few times I had mishaps."
-"What kind of mishaps? Did you beam into objects?"
-"No, that's kind of impossible. You can only beam to where you can see. But there were times it didn't work at all and sometimes I only moved a few inches forward."

*

This new ability made me very curious. "How far does this work? Any distance?"

"Exactly one mile," José answered. "There is a distance limit."

I was a little disappointed by that answer, I admit. Why a mile, of all distances? Who said so? Without meaning to, I stared into space and beamed a mile up.

The landing was painful.

Pain in Heaven is relative. Ordinary behavior shouldn't cause pain. Nor should jumping or collisions. But if you like pain, you'll feel it. Because it is a kind of pleasure. But real pain, harsh pain, shouldn't exist. Only in extreme incidents. A long enough drop will hurt. Even hurt very much.

"Good, good," José explained after he scraped me off the jagged rock I had crashed onto. "That's how you learn your boundaries, which is why you won't push the rules to the limit."

Again, rules. I didn't like it. Why would Heaven have rules?

"Anywhere there are people, you need rules." Jackie added her two cents to the conversation. "You can get up."

I didn't feel like I could, but I got up anyway. Indeed, no bones were broken and there were no scrapes on my skin. After a few steps, the sharp pain started to fade as well. But the rules worked, apparently, and the lesson stayed with me. I didn't stare up into the air unintentionally anymore.

After half an hour, we reached the pub.

MEMORY 2

The mist came, the mist went away.

We were there, the two of us, Mommy and I. Hand in hand. She was very big and I was very small. The pit was very deep. I wanted to ask her why we were there, but she cried all day and I knew my little question would make her cry more. I looked around. There were other people around me. They were all big. I was the only child; they were all taking an interest in my well-being. I looked at the pit. Why had they dug a hole here? The people were next to the soldiers. Daddy was a soldier too, I knew it. Maybe these people were his friends.

It could be.

Some of them looked at me. Those whose glances I caught turned away from me quickly. They whispered among themselves. One of them pointed at me, but he hurried to hide the movement when I caught him looking. I looked up at Mommy. She was still crying, still blowing her nose every now and then. I let go of her hand. I approached the edge of the pit, looking in. Why did they dig such a big hole here? And if so, where were the bucket and shovel? Because I wanted to play too.

But I was sad.

I waited for Daddy. I hadn't seen him for a long time. I wanted to see him. All of a sudden, all the adults looked at me. Suddenly I grew cold. Suddenly it became quiet. Some of the men had rifles. They aimed them up into the air and fired. They were soldiers. Daddy was a soldier too, I knew it, but he wasn't with them. I felt like something bad was going to happen.

The mist came, the mist went away.

THE PUB

We arrived at the pub at night.

No, the sun didn't go down. It was night because, at that particular place, it was just night. At the same place, always night. And it was always a wonderful night, smelling good, starry. With bats flying among the dark treetops, a comet blazing in the sky, and an amazing orange moon, impossibly huge.

The pub was situated inside a large cave carved into a low mountain. Over the entrance was a big holo-sign, medieval style, showing a leprechaun dressed in green and drinking beer, sitting on a golden barrel. Every now and then a rainbow appeared out of the barrel and reached for the sky, flickered twice, and disappeared.

The entrance was through classic pub doors, swinging on hinges. The scent of alcohol and cigarette smoke wafted out, accompanied by typical pub music. I thought I recognized an old classic of 1D. Or was it U2? I could never really differentiate between the two.

"Are you coming?" Jackie asked after noticing I was lingering behind.

I came.

The music was substantially louder once we were inside. It was hard to hear each other, the smoke made it hard to see, and it was quite crowded.

Not that I was suffering. This was still Heaven, after all, and cigarettes were apparently acceptable here. They had an amazing aroma and caused zero damage. The music was high quality, and almost seemed as if it was coming right out of your head. In a way, it sort of was. As for the crowdedness... it made it so that I was constantly touched. Pleasant touches, accompanied by inviting smiles, with minimal clothing.

Jackie grabbed my hand and pulled me forward. We found a vacant table at the end of the bar and, within seconds, a smiling waitress was standing next to us. What does a waitress do in Heaven? Takes orders, of course. Guinness for José, Bushmills for Jackie, and for me.... Honestly, I didn't know what to order. I couldn't remember what I liked.

"Give him a Bushmills, too," Jackie instructed the waitress, who eyed me carefully before she left.

*

-*"Bushmills. How long has it been since they stopped making it?"*
-*"In Heaven it exists. Pretty much all European drinks still exist. Italian wines, Scots whiskey…."*
-*"Nostalgic. So how's the taste?"*
-*"Like the pineapple. It might be called by the same name as it is downstairs, maybe the taste is even a little reminiscent, but that's where the similarities end. It's so much better!"*

*

"Okay, so what is this place?" I demanded to know after the waitress had left.

"The Leprechaun," José answered. "One of the best pubs."

"Why are there pubs in Heaven?"

They exchanged glances again, each hinting at the other to start first. "You explain it, lollipop. He'll understand more quickly," José urged his wife. She nodded, sighed, and focused her attention on me.

I felt myself starting to get excited. Her eyes were big and clear, her cheekbones were well defined. And I noticed that she, in her cheetah way, was very beautiful. She smiled and everything became much more pleasant. Above all, she was about to tell me something I didn't know. Something important.

"You don't remember anything from when you were alive?"

"Nothing. I told you. Not even one little detail."

"And what about the world? What happened in Europe? The Caliphate?"

I took a moment to think. Yes, I knew what was going on in the world. I knew Europe was a ridge of ruins, I knew about the Caliphate and the new Jihad, I knew about Japan, and I knew about Russia and China. I also knew about what was going on in the United States of America, about the wave of Christian refugees, about the Newborn. I nodded my head.

That satisfied her. She took a deep breath, started to say something, paused, then started again.

"Okay, look. You're not in Heaven. I mean, not the fairy-tale Heaven, or religious Heaven. It's -"

"That's U2," I interrupted her, completely surprised I was able to recognize the band.

"What?"

"This is an old U2 song, am I right?"

She nodded her head. But I was very excited.

"How do I know it's U2? I'm not supposed to know anything! Maybe my memory's coming back to me?"

"Maybe... but I don't think that's the reason..."

"What do you mean, no? It's a well-known fact that music brings back memories. And I obviously love U2, or else how would I know it was U2? They're an Irish rock band! One of the most successful ever, active at the end of the twentieth century and two decades be..."

My voice died.

Deep inside I realized that wasn't how a real person who loves a rock band would speak. It sounded exactly like...

"Pedia," Jackie said. "That is information from the Pedia. The info's built into the system here. It has nothing to do with your personal memories."

I kept quiet. Took another sip of my Bushmills (a blended Irish whiskey brand, made continuously since 1608 using the same methods and recipes), and then I stayed silent for a little longer.

"What system are you talking about?" I asked quietly.

"Heaven," she replied, also quietly. "It's not the Heaven you thought. It's..."

"It's digital." I suddenly knew. "It's not real. An illusion."

"It's not an illusion, it's not. It's completely real for us."

"You're not real either. You only exist in my imagination."

A wave of cold sweat took over my body. Suddenly, I felt all was lost. I was sure I'd had an accident. Yes, yes. I was probably somewhere in a hospital, unconscious. Perhaps there was a whole team of doctors trying to resuscitate me. Perhaps I was just thrown onto the side of the road and was waiting to die. Perhaps I was a captive of the Caliphate and they were experimenting on me. Maybe -

"You're wrong." José interrupted my morbid thoughts. "This is not in your imagination and it is completely real."

Jackie nodded and they kissed, which made me even more upset. "But it's not real," I insisted. "You're a computer program! You're just... a digital recording of a brain!"

"And what are you?" he shot back. "You feel real to yourself?"

-*"It doesn't change the feeling completely, when you know you're not real."*
-*"But I am real."*
-*"No, you're not."*
-*"Let's not argue about it now. I felt completely real. I still feel like that."*

*

"You think, therefore you exist," said some ancient philosopher I refused to check on the Pedia. There was no doubt I existed. From the moment I rose to Heaven I was packed with thoughts, opinions, sensations, emotions. Yes, emotions.

"Emotions are thoughts, too," said Jackie, and woke me up completely.

"But I didn't say that out loud," I said in a loud, bitter voice.

They looked at each other again, as if they were two heads of a frustrated dragon.

"Don't pretend you don't know what I'm talking about. This trash has happened a few times. I thought of something and you answered my thoughts directly. The conclusion is obvious: You are not real. I'm dreaming you. I must be lying somewhere, unconscious, and this whole thing is - ouch!"

Jackie pinched my nipple. Pinched so hard I thought it was going to fall off.

"That doesn't mean anything," I blurted out, rubbing the sore spot. "So I dreamed you pinched me. In dreams, unexpected things happen."

"The man in the cave." José chuckled. I knew it was another philosophical reference and I refused to check it. Ignorance suddenly looked like a pretty good shelter. Especially since this pub was carved into a cave, which didn't seem like a coincidence at that moment. "Listen, hmm…. I don't know what to call you. Dude. Noob. Although you should be at least ninety."

I tried to interrupt, but he raised his hand and silenced me. His eyes were angry.

"The reason we can read your mind is that the system understands them as part of our conversation. We're in Heaven, for Heaven's sake. Like you said, we don't really have bodies and we don't really talk, or drink the best trashing Bushmills ever made!"

He paused for a breath and then continued, "When you think you're talking, you aren't really talking. You're just moving some quantums from side to side in your core code. When you think you're thinking, the same thing happens. I don't even know what parts you're thinking about and what parts you're saying out loud. To me it all sounds out loud, understand?"

*

-"I needed another bottle."
-"And did you get one?"
-"Sure. It's Heaven."

*

Heaven or not, the whiskey had the same influence here. When we left The Leprechaun, the air continued to be sweet and chilly, the night continued to be perfect and dark, and the moon continued to capture hearts. I was drunk and the world spun around me nicely. I sat on the grass and they looked at me, worried.

"Are you really dead?" I asked Jackie.

"José died from lung cancer in 2111. Luckily, we were rich enough to fund his ascent to Heaven. We sold our houses, everything. The kids helped too. It wasn't a process that could be come by easily back in those days, and it didn't always work. But José survived the process and came up here. After a couple of years he convinced me to join him, even though I was healthy."

José smiled. "It wasn't easy. She's a stubborn one, as you've noticed."

"How did you convince her, really? You were here and she was down there. Still alive."

"It's different from a regular death," Jackie answered for him. "I was already ninety and so many friends were dying around me. Permanent death. Like the old days. But José... it was like he had just left on a trip. We talked every day. Sometimes a few times a day. I didn't feel like others around me felt. And he constantly mind-trashed me on how good it was here and that I should come to him."

"What baloney!" José interjected. "It was you who wanted to come, after you saw I was young and beautiful again."

33

"Well, what did you expect? How could I have stayed old, when you were jumping around like a young goat, the same age as our grandchildren?"

They blew each other a kiss in the air. I rolled my eyes.

"But how did you talk? I mean specifically how. He was here and you were... there."

"Bounce back from your whiskey. We'll show you."

*

-"Twenty minutes later we beamed together to the Plain of Souls."
-"The what?"
-"The Plain of Souls. Where I'm at right now."

*

The Plain of Souls was completely different from the forest and the cave. It was a desert, utterly flat and in a permanent state of twilight, with crimson skies and occasional lightning. ("This is what it's always like here," said Jackie.) Thunder rumbled in the distance, supplying a steady soundtrack. The noise did not disrupt the chatter, but sent out a creepy vibe through the whole area. A combination between a horror holo and a visit to a holy place.

And there were souls there. Thousands of them, all glowing white.

"It's just the light coming from downstairs that makes them look white," José explained when we passed next to one of them. It was a rather short man, perhaps six feet, with Asian features. He was absorbed in looking down into the ground, occasionally mumbling something while lightly gesturing with his hands.

I tried to go near him, but José put a furry hand on my chest. "That's rude," he said. "He's probably talking to his children or someone else down there."

"We'll show you," said Jackie when she saw my brows furrow. "Here - an unoccupied well."

We were standing next to something that resembled an ancient well, a circle of charred red bricks, a little over four feet in diameter, around a dark hole in the ground. I leaned over, trying to see how deep it went, but it was too dark.

"Now, watch." Jackie smiled and the well lit up.

The light almost hurt my eyes. White, bright, solid. "I hope someone's home," she said. "This is an unplanned visit. Let's hope someone answers." It took a few seconds, but someone did answer. The holo showed a young man, overly tattooed, with a band of piercings on his face and a shiny bald head, dyed purple. He looked up at us.

"Hey, Grandpa, Grandma," he said in a hoarse voice. "Long time..."

"I know, Earl. That's how it is here, you lose track of time. How's everything? Did that test work out?"

"Which one? The one from two years ago?"

"Ah... yes."

"Actually, I failed, but it doesn't matter. I'm not counting much on the degree. Who's that guy next to you? He looks like coal."

The purple, tattooed guy looked straight at me and suddenly, for the first time since I had come up to Heaven, I felt naked. In a negative way. Suddenly I realized I, too, probably had grandchildren somewhere on Earth... downstairs. And if not grandchildren, then at least children, still living down there. Maybe they were looking for me? Perhaps they were waiting for a sign of life from me?

I felt guilty. Jackie and José had been dead for over sixty years, but had never really left their family. They kept in touch, they took an interest, and they were still alive... in a way.

What about my children? I had only been dead for a few days, that's all. They were probably expecting me to call. To let them know. Maybe they were worried sick down there. It was probably not a cheap process, getting up to Heaven. Not everyone could. Probably only very wealthy, or very important, people could go where I had inexplicably arrived. So my children were waiting for me. Probably worried. Perhaps even mad. Maybe they would sue the system? And if they sued, what would happen to me here?

One thing was certain. I had to find out who I was—and fast.

"That's our friend," Jackie answered and looked at me for a moment. "He's new here. His name is... his name is Black."

"Because of his color? Come on."

"He chose the color, we picked the name."

"Good for him, at least he died in time."

"What do you mean?"

"I can tell you haven't visited in years. And why would you, really? I'm referring to the Caliphate fanatics and the trashing Newborn."

*

-"Talk about detachment!"

-"Yeah, after you go up to Heaven, there isn't always a reason to keep in touch with those downstairs."

-"But... I thought that was the main reason to go up to Heaven."

-"Maybe. But when you're actually here, things look different."

-"How strange."

-"When you're here, it's not that unusual."

-"So... it was the first time you heard about the Newborn?"

*

"It's because of those lunatics you should finish your degree. The world needs talented Bionaotics."

"Hmm, yes." Earl hesitated and then looked up courageously, his head held high. "I thought about enlisting."

Jackie stomped her foot on the ground. It was clear to me this was a sensitive subject. José just turned around and moved out of sight, mumbling curses at the ground. I had no doubt there were some juicy words in there, but all I heard was, "Trash, trash, trash-trash."

"Don't you understand?" Jackie eventually said. "Those who enlist could simply die! There's no supervision! How will you get to Heaven that way?"

"There are more important things than eternal life."

"Oh, don't talk nonsense. We worked a lot of years to have money for the whole family to come here. I won't permit you to enlist."

Now it was Earl's turn to get frustrated. He raised his hands up and smacked them down on his waist, huffing angrily. The piercings covering his face clattered. After ten seconds, he was finally able to answer.

"Someone has to look out for you two, you know. Your eternal life won't be very long, otherwise."

José heard this and hurried back into the well's line of sight, pushing Jackie aside.

"This place is supposed to be protected!" He jabbed his finger in the air in his rage.

"And Europe was supposed to stay Christian!" yelled Earl.

The words echoed in the air for a few seconds, eventually fading into silence. Jackie and José didn't know how to answer him. After a

36

few more seconds of silence, Earl's gaze softened.

"Listen." He tried to reason with them. "You know that just last week there was a rough battle at the entrance of the compound?"

"We heard nothing about it. Someone must have accidentally fired a shot. These incidents have been happening for decades."

"This time it's different. The Newborn are a lot more organized today. They mean business."

José did not look like someone who believed his grandson's words, but something in his body language changed nevertheless. His hands dropped to his sides. His fists clenched.

"So the terrorists won?" he asked in a quivering voice.

"If they'd won, we wouldn't be talking today -"

"So, you see?" José interrupted, but Earl raised his voice and stubbornly continued his sentence.

"- But they managed to booby-trap one of the supply trucks, and after it blew up they came in helicopters…"

"Helicopters? Where did they get helicopters from?"

I heard concern in José's voice. His cheetah forehead wrinkled a little. He scratched his head. I had questions, many questions, but I felt it was better that I stand aside, be quiet, and listen. Especially to Earl, who seemed a lot more connected to reality.

"They're military surplus. There are rumors about a wave of desertion…"

"Now you're just talking nonsense! We've heard nothing about it."

"Because you two are deaf! Now I guess you're going to tell me you haven't heard about the battles in Boulder."

"What battles?"

Earl's eyes widened in disbelief. He turned around, trying to find the words. His face was soon flushed a deep crimson.

"You guys are just unreal. You haven't heard? The Newborn have carried out assaults on a few of the neighborhoods where Heaven's workers live. There were dozens killed! I could hear the shots from my balcony!"

José turned a questioning gaze toward Jackie. She shrugged and shook her head. She didn't know anything about it either.

"Can I ask a question?" I interrupted carefully.

Earl looked at me, then back to Jackie. She nodded. "He's okay," she said.

"Ask away."

"Who are the Newborn?"

37

José burst out with a sad laugh. Jackie's jaw dropped. Earl raised his purple brows.

"Are you for real?"

Once again, I felt like the new guy at the party, who doesn't understand what the conversation is about and what exactly everyone is laughing at. And when that happens to you, as you know, they're probably laughing at you. I had no choice but to speak the truth.

"I'm sorry. I'm just new here, and nothing about the Newborn exists in the Pedia."

José stopped laughing. His eyes focused on a point in the distance, as if he was trying to think of something but couldn't.

"He's right. There's nothing about them in the Pedia." He turned to Jackie. "Can you find anything?"

"Nothing," she said.

"Perhaps a malfunction?"

Jackie returned a sad smile and shook her head. "No."

"Now it makes sense why you haven't heard," said Earl. "They don't want you to know what's really happening."

"So what is really happening?" I brought his attention back to me. "Who the trash are the Newborn?"

"Basically, they're religious men who object to Heaven," Earl explained, after letting out an impatient huff. "They think the whole idea is blasphemy."

"Lousy terrorists," José barked out in fury and kicked at a pebble nearby. "A negligible minority, nothing to fear."

"They're not so negligible anymore, Grandpa. I told you, just last week they -"

"Yeah, yeah, I heard. That's bullshit."

Earl shrugged, understanding there was no point in adding anything more. I personally had many more questions, but it was not my conversation. And he changed the subject.

"Say, are Mom and Dad around?"

"No," said Jackie. "I haven't seen them in months. I think he's still on his journey to Moria and she's working on some ecological project."

"Alright… tell them to contact me. I miss them, and the little guys want to see them, too."

"We'll let them know. Bye for now, Earl."

"Bye," he said, and the well darkened.

-"A difficult conversation."

-"Yes. If there was a moment when I finally understood where I really was, it was then."

-"Welcome to reality."

-"I'd rather not. And there was something else. For the first time since I had gotten to Heaven, I thought not just of myself, but of the world I'd left behind."

-"That's exciting."

-"And then I went back to thinking about myself."

*

"Are your children still alive? Or are they here too?"

I asked that after we had moved away a little. We were still on the Plain of Souls. I wanted to get the feel of the place a little, to experience it. That's not something you can do if you just beam out. So we walked, even though the Johnsons—that was their last name, apparently—grumbled a little.

"Our daughter, Elvira," Jackie explained. "And her idiot husband."

"He's not such an idiot, my stevia."

"He is, and stop defending him. Only an idiot spends that much time in Moria instead of doing useful things like our Elvira."

"I don't know," José continued. "Sometimes a man needs to just go and clear his mind. Besides, you have to admit, it's pretty fun, with all the orcs and the -"

"And the what?" I interrupted. "What orcs, exactly?"

I was shocked. I had not yet processed the whole Newborn thing and now this. Who were the orcs anyway? Another religious faction I didn't know about?

"The orcs of Moria," he answered patiently. "What other orcs would there be?"

They exchanged another look. I was getting tired of being the one who didn't know anything about what was going on around him. For a moment I wanted to connect to the Pedia, but didn't; I wasn't feeling comfortable enough to do that yet. I wanted them to tell me. I wanted someone human—more or less— to explain all this nonsense to me.

"You know Tolkien?"

I did.

"Well, they brought his world to Heaven. Middle-earth. Moria is the place where the dwarfs lived, but then they had a disaster and -"

"I know what Moria is," I interrupted. "And you can visit there?"

"You can live there, too. In fact, there are quite a few people who just live there. Dreamers, we call them. It's a very popular place."

I promised myself that I would do go there at some point.

"Are there other places like that in Heaven?"

Jackie smiled. "Yes. But tell me, aren't you tired?"

I yawned.

THE CITY

We went on our way to their home.

To reach it, we beamed for almost half an hour straight. A moment before we reached their hometown, Midlake City, I paused to look at it from a distance. It sat at the center of an emerald lake surrounded by marble-pink mountains. Breathtaking. The city was made up of hundreds of buildings built from the same pink stone. They towered thousands of feet high, narrow and round, and each floor was surrounded by a terrace, from which lively green plants extended downward.

There were other buildings too, wider and shorter. Some of those were built from the pink stone, but there were also buildings the color of deep jade. The contrasting colors and singular architecture created an otherworldly harmony.

The lake itself was full of life. With one look I saw hundreds of people swimming, water-skiing, and paragliding. Others surfed the perfect waves like experts, and although the waves formed only in front of one beach, they peaked to several dozen feet. I watched the surfers with envy. Soon I would join them, I promised myself. But after I rested.

There was no apparent bridge reaching over the lake into the city. To reach it you had to beam in.

That didn't work quite as I expected.

*

-"What did you feel?"
-"Massive pain. White, blinding light. And I swallowed water."

*

For a few seconds I was simply paralyzed from the pain. I couldn't move any part of my body, including my lungs and my eyes. I just sank farther down, motionless, into the lake. It was very deep. The water grew bluer; a few silver swordfish gathered around me and looked at me curiously. I sank like a basalt rock, deeper and deeper.

41

The pressure in my ears grew stronger and far off in the distance I saw something that looked like one of those prehistoric sea monsters that are featured on so many neuro shows these days. Its teeth were too long for my liking.

After fifteen seconds of free-falling into the lake, the pain began to pass and with it the paralysis. My lungs started working again—and I instinctively breathed in water. It was a horrible feeling. I coughed, still under water, then stopped breathing and started kicking my arms and legs with wild, powerful motions. Somehow, without aiming, I swam up.

I came out over the waves, coughing and choking. My heart was beating wildly, pumped full of adrenaline, while my brain tried to calm it down. After all, I was not really in danger. What danger could there be in Heaven? Nevertheless, the sensation had been eerily similar to real drowning.

A man on a silver jet ski stopped next to me, causing a big wave.

"Are you okay?" he asked.

As a response, I coughed twice. He reached out a strong hand, grabbed my arm, and pulled me up onto the back of the jet ski. In my heart, I was thanking him, but water kept draining out of my mouth, nose, and ears, so a real thank you would have to wait. While the rest of the water poured from my various orifices, I noticed my rescuer was completely nude. This was standard here, as I had already come to realize. His nakedness, at least, seemed pretty ordinary—nothing exaggerated or inhuman, like cheetah fur. He was relatively short, with long red hair and such ordinary facial features that they looked like they might have been from his previous life.

"I saw you stop in midair and plummet down," he continued. "What happened?"

I still couldn't talk, so I just shrugged and kept returning the liquid I had borrowed back to the lake. In the meantime a few more people gathered around us, some swimmers, some paragliders, and one mermaid with a big golden fin. They started talking amongst themselves excitedly, occasionally addressing a question to me, none of which I knew how to answer.

It turned out that as Jackie and José had beamed into the city normally, I had bumped into some invisible barrier that seemed to be surrounding it. Once it had been triggered, it appeared as a glowing dome over the city. From what I heard around me, this was quite a bizarre occurrence, since no one had been aware of the barrier's existence.

"Wait - the city's closed? Someone tried to beam in?" someone asked. In response, some people looked at the city and beamed into it, then out, then back in, and then back out.

Those attempts appeared to calm everyone's nerves. The problem was not the city, but me.

"You have to tell us who you really are," someone declared. It was a muscular-looking man wearing a scuba diving suit and carrying a bloody pitchfork.

The rest of the crowd looked at him with a mix of anger and shock.

*

-"Why?"

-"Apparently it's unacceptable to ask that. It's forbidden."

-"What? That doesn't make sense. How do you find your relatives up there, if you don't ask?"

-"Although a lot of people keep in touch with each other after they go up to Heaven, a lot decide to cut their ties."

-"That's the first time I've heard about it."

-"That just shows how little you understand. Death is a wonderful opportunity to wipe the slate clean. When you go up, you say good-bye to everything you were downstairs. You leave everything, pick a shiny new body... is there any better way to reinvent yourself? Your image?"

-"Why would someone want to change their... never mind. I get it."

-"So it's considered rude to demand to know someone's previous identity. In fact, it's fairly rude to tell about it, too."

*

"What right do you have to demand that of him?" a blue-haired windsurfer raged at the man with the pitchfork. He answered hatefully, she yelled back at him, and then more people jumped into the argument. From what I could work out, they were once siblings, heirs to billions from a big energy company, and they had carried their unfinished business upstairs. At some point she slapped him and he tried to stab her with the pitchfork. The others jumped in and separated them, and it looked like they had almost completely forgotten about me, until a bold Buddhist monk with an orange robe

43

and a yellow face pointed at me and spoke loudly but calmly.

"It's really important and relevant information. We need to know what triggered this."

The whole group quietened down and looked at me. Pitchfork man shot a smug glance at his sister.

"I don't know who I am," I answered simply.

Grumbles of disappointment came from the crowd and then new arguments and yelling began. Most of this was directed toward me, not to mention unpleasant hints in my direction from the pitchfork man.

"But I really don't know who I am!" I tried to explain to the monk. He wouldn't listen. Instead, he started preaching in a calm voice about how I was endangering the people here with my silly secrecy and how all life in Heaven was ruined because secrecy was even allowed.

"In the real Heaven, only pure people are meant to be there," he declared. "Not politicians and tycoons."

A gentle-looking woman tried to defend me. "Maybe he lost his memory in the fall? Or perhaps it's from the lightning..."

"No," I blurted without thinking. "It's from when I arrived here. I came up here with no memory."

That bit of information created a new enthusiastic cacophony. As I already knew, this was unheard of.

"How can someone come up here with no memory, it's digitally impossible!"

"Such rubbish!"

"I guess he does have something to hide!"

"He had it coming!"

Those were only some of the comments I heard. A number of people abandoned me and went back about their business. My savior started to look impatient.

"Listen, are you okay? Have you recuperated?"

"I think so."

"Then, if you don't mind, maybe -"

At that moment the Johnsons beamed to us.

*

-"Wait. This whole time, they were inside the city?"

-"Yes. And because they came back, I really started to like them. They didn't

have to come back, you see."
-"Good folks."
-"Yes. Much to their regret."

*

"Black!" José addressed me. Jackie pounced on my savior and gave him a heartwarming embrace. "What happened to you? Where did you disappear to?"

"You know him?" asked the savior.

"Yes, he's with us. What happened?"

"He couldn't beam in. He smacked into this dome over the city. Hey, you guys were one of the first ones here - did you know such a thing existed?"

José looked back to the city. He didn't see anything unusual.

"There's no such thing."

"It's new to us, too," Jackie confirmed. She turned to me. "Are you okay?"

"I almost drowned."

She smiled and tried to say something, but I didn't let her. "Yes, I know I can't drown here, but that was how it felt!"

My savior looked at Jackie, a questioning look in his eyes.

"Is he really new here?"

She shrugged. "He didn't even know how to beam before we found him."

"Wow. Where did you find him?"

"At El-Paso," she said. José gave her a piercing look, like he was trying to tell her something. She hesitated for a second and then continued. "He had just left the entrance and climbed the trees there."

My savior smiled understandingly. "Well, we all do that at first... it's the pineapples." He extended his hand. "Dave. Dave Sharky."

His hand looked very small, but his handshake was firm and steady. "Nice to meet you. And thank you for helping me. I have no name," I apologized.

"We call him Black," José supplied.

"Black is nice. Welcome to Heaven."

"Good to be here. I think."

I yawned again. I started to feel the fatigue José had mentioned earlier. Without a doubt, I needed some rest.

"It's safe to say," Sharky said with a hint of skepticism, "that ninety-nine percent of humanity would trade places with you. Don't worry. If you're here, there must be someone taking care of you."

José smacked his forehead.

"How did I not think about this earlier!" said José. "To come up to Heaven, you have to have someone downstairs! A son, a grandson, a wife, a lawyer. And it's not cheap to come up here."

"Yes, they must be looking for me!" I almost jumped off the jet ski. "So how can I find them?"

"Oh, you just have to get into the city, then the system will recognize you auto... oh."

Awkward silence.

Eventually José went back to his train of thought. "You can't go in, so the system can't identify you."

"I think it's the other way around," I corrected him. "Because the system doesn't recognize me, I can't enter the city."

All three nodded.

"Perhaps we could try to get into the city without beaming?"

José had brilliant ideas sometimes.

*

-"So you tried?"
-"Of course we tried."
-"Did you succeed?"

*

"I've never seen anything like this," Jackie said angrily after a few tries. All three - José, Jackie, and Dave - were in the safe zone, an arm's length away from me. But I was outside, and frustrated.

I leaned against the barrier again. Its texture was a little like glass. It was impenetrable, cold, and transparent. Only when I touched it did it come to life with a little show of fireworks. The feeling when I attempted to push through was tingling and thorny, like petting staticky cat fur on a particularly dry day. But penetrate it? I couldn't.

I tried to push myself in a few times, and one not so clever time I tried again to beam in. It hurt just like the last time, only this time I wasn't taken by surprise. Of course, I didn't have a chance to drown before the Johnsons pulled me up onto Dave's jet ski. They told me the city's defensive dome had completely lit up again.

I looked at the city streets from the outside. They were practically empty.

"What am I missing, not going into the city?"

"Not much," said Jackie. "We mostly come here to sleep."

José disagreed with her. "But that's exactly the point, my eucalyptus honey—sleep!"

They both had a serious look on their face. I didn't understand why.

"I can sleep outside too," I said. I couldn't remember if I had been a camping sort of person in my past, but how hard could it be in Heaven? It wasn't like hungry crocodiles roamed around here or that it was too cold to fall asleep. But then the real problem suddenly dawned on me. "Why exactly do you have to sleep here?"

*

-"Why?"

-"Because living means gathering information. Because downstairs, your eyes are open sixteen hours a day and your ears hear twenty-four hours a day. The nose smells. The mouth tastes. Each cell of your skin absorbs information from your surroundings, reporting temperature, pressure, and so on. Not to mention hunger receptors or bladder pressure. It's a lot of information to process, remember, and keep."

-"But we don't remember everything. The mind doesn't keep irrelevant information."

-"In Heaven, everything is kept."

-"Heaven is based on quantum computerization. There's no limit to the amount of information you can keep."

-"But there is a limit to the speed at which you can draw from it. Because you're absorbing information, endlessly. Who cares what the pineapple at El Paso tasted like? Or how many leaves you saw on the tree there? Or any tree! But it's information, regardless. And it is kept."

-"So irrelevant information needs to be erased."

-"Exactly! And don't forget that there are hundreds of thousands of people in Heaven."

-"Millions, now."

-"So - millions. Each one of them accumulates information at an alarming rate. To keep functioning, there must be a way to unload, process, analyze, and compress it."

"So, basically, I have to sleep?" I asked José.

"Technically, yes. We all get tired every now and then and go home to unload."

"And if you don't come back home?"

Jackie and José exchanged glances.

"That's never happened to us," Jackie said carefully. "It's also never happened to anyone we know of. Do you remember anyone giving up on sleep, Dave?"

"No," he said. "When you get tired, you go sleep for a few hours and that's it."

"What about people who go on adventures?" I tried. "The ones in Tolkien's books?"

"They have a place to sleep too. Listen, you don't have to go to sleep every day. But once every few days is recommended."

"So I'll ask you again: What if I don't?"

Silence.

"There's no reason for that to happen," Jackie finally said. "Let's go see the mayor."

"There's a mayor here?"

"Yeah, he's cute. We'll bring him here."

*

-"I've heard about the mayors in Heaven. They're…"

-"Exactly. And this one in particular took a long time to get there. In the meantime, what really worried me was the whole Newborn thing."

-"Hah. Rightly so."

-"Yes. But what scared me most about it was the censorship. I didn't like the fact that there were people who wanted to kill me, despite me already being dead, but I liked that they were trying to hide it from me even less."

*

I looked around. People were partying and laughing, jumping up in the air and diving underwater, not to mention the other things they did, both privately and publicly. The air was sweet, the fruits divine, the sky amazing, and in the background an enormous rainbow decorated the sky. By all appearances everything was perfect. But something in the air reminded me of the neuro feeds from Rome just before its destruction, New York before World War III, and Paris before the dirty bomb.

After ten minutes José and Jackie beamed back, accompanied by an angry, middle-aged man. He had gray hair, a gray suit, a gray folding chair, and a gray briefcase. He didn't waste time on manners and immediately sat on the folding chair and opened the briefcase. Inside was a gray screen on which he started tapping his finger.

"Name?" he asked, without even looking at me.

"Black." And after a split second, "Royal Black."

The mayor lifted a questioning gaze to me.

"Was that your name downstairs?"

"I don't remember."

"Seriously now?"

"I am serious. I truly don't remember."

The mayor looked at me, surprised, then looked at the Johnsons.

"I see. Can you two give us a moment?" he asked.

They both nodded and then beamed into the lake, where they started splashing water at each other like children.

"You can speak freely now," the mayor said. "No one will hear your little secret."

"But I don't have a secret. I really don't remember."

"Perhaps no one explained this to you," he continued patiently, "but anything you say to me is confidential and will not be shared with any of the other residents here. Even if I wanted to tell them something, I couldn't. So… go on."

"Listen, the reason you're here now is to help me find out who I am! Didn't they tell you?"

The mayor looked over at the Johnsons. "They did, but I never believe people. They tend to lie."

"Well, I don't know who I am. I swear."

"There, you see?" The mayor smiled at me. "Lies."

Patience, apparently, wasn't my strong suit. I kept explaining to him that I didn't know who I was and he continued to try to explain to me that I was a liar. It wouldn't have been so bad if he had at least checked. I just wanted to know who I was, and his stupidity infuriated me. So the tone of my voice got higher and higher until eventually I heard myself screaming.

The Johnsons beamed back with worried faces, both completely wet.

"What's going on?" Jackie asked.

I couldn't answer her. I was that mad.

"Your friend refuses to tell me who he is," the mayor continued patiently.

"He doesn't know who he is. That's part of the problem."

"You know that's impossible. Identity is an inseparable part of you."

"Well the fact remains, it happened. Can you not just check for yourself to see who he is? Identify him in the system?"

The mayor looked like he had just cracked the secret of the universe. "Of course! Why didn't you ask sooner? Give me your hand." He reached his hand out, but then pulled it back just as I extended mine.

"I'm not allowed to do this," he said. "Only by your explicit request. Do you wish to expose your original identity to me?"

"I do, I'm asking!"

His handshake was cold, stern, and short.

I looked at him, full of hope.

SABERTOOTH

"Now all becomes clear," the mayor sighed, relieved. "He's just an AI."

José's jaw dropped, amazed.

"He can't be an AI," said Jackie. "He's a real person, like me. Like everyone here."

"You can think what you want, but you cannot argue with the data in our archives." The mayor was adamant. "He is an AI, well programmed, but completely AI."

The three of them looked at me. The mayor impatiently, the Johnsons with something between anger and shock.

*

-*"But you're not an AI."*

-*"Of course not. And to think that not that long ago I, myself, had thought the Johnsons were AI, and that this whole world was one big AI going on in my head."*

-*"How could he be so wrong?"*

*

"Artificial intelligence," José muttered. "You got me good, I must admit."

When I'm angry, I have trouble speaking. This accusation that I was an AI pissed me off more than anything thus far. Say I'm new, call me young, tell me I don't have a clue - but don't you dare say I'm an artificial intelligence. I am not a machine, I'm not a program. I exist like any other person. I think, therefore I am. Simple as that.

As I searched for words, Jackie found them.

"Yes, Royal," she said sadly, "that explains everything. You have no memory of who you were downstairs because you were never there."

José clenched his fists. "This is unbelievable! Is this how you trick people?" he yelled at the mayor. "Do you know how much time we've invested in him? Guiding him, taking him…"

His face was very close to the mayor's and with each word spit sprayed from his mouth. But for some reason it didn't bother the mayor. He just stood there, completely serene, nodding his head in empathy.

Jackie, in the meantime, had started stroking my hand. She didn't ask permission, she didn't do it discreetly, she didn't even pretend that I had a choice in the matter. She just took my muscular hand and started stroking.

Although the sensation itself was pleasant, the reason for it was not.

"I'm not an AI!" I pushed her hands away from me. "I'm a real person!"

"There's no doubt there must be some malfunction here," the mayor apologized to José, ignoring me completely.

"This is not a malfunction! This is an outrage!"

José's face was set like stone and he crossed his arms on his chest. "I want to know what you're going to do about this."

The mayor sighed and turned to me.

"I'm asking you to end now."

I think my brows went so high up, they left my face completely. I fought my growing desire to punch the gray old man right in the nose. Instead, I turned to the Johnsons, who were looking at me with anticipation. Probably expecting me to vanish into thin air or something.

"Tell me, is he serious?" I yelled.

"Actually, he's also an AI," Jackie answered. "And you have to do what he asks, unfortunately."

The mayor got up off his chair and stood before me, exuding a calm strength that was indisputable. He looked deep into my eyes. "I am asking you again. End. Now."

I punched him in the face. Hard.

*

-"Yes! That's what you should have done to begin with!"

-"I think that until that moment, I hadn't really realized how strong I was. I mean, I saw my muscles and I could feel that my body was strong. I figured the punch would stun him, or knock him back a few steps. Or back a few dozen steps."

-"How far did you actually knock him back?"

52

-"That's not exactly the right question."

*

My fist sank deep into the gray head and vanished.

For a brief moment, the mayor just stood there, stunned. Then he shattered. Scattered into endless little gray fragments as if he was made of glass. His particles hovered in the air for a split second and then fell down to the ground like a little hail storm.

Jackie squealed and then brought her hand to her mouth. José took a step back fearfully. Then he pulled Jackie close, hugging her.

I was just as shocked. My hand remained in midair, like it didn't know what to do next. It felt weird, like I had punched through a concrete wall. On the one hand, my knuckles hurt very much, but on the other hand, it wasn't a bad kind of pain. I felt like finally my hand had done something it was meant to do.

I looked at it for a moment. My fist was still clenched, with not even a scratch, wound, or any other evidence of the fact that it had just busted a man into tiny little pieces. I looked at José and Jackie. As one, they took a small step back.

"What... what did you do to him?" José's voice shook.

It was the first time I saw the Johnsons fear me. I brought my hand back to my side, hiding it from them. I didn't want them to be scared of me.

"I don't know. I just wanted him to leave me alone. Did I end him?"

José looked at the gray remains. "It doesn't look like it. When an AI ends, it just... disappears."

Hmm.

"So I might have killed him?"

"He's just an AI. You can't kill him."

"No one's ever tried," Jackie added over her husband's words. She looked a little less stressed and her words made me very curious.

"So you're saying that if he'd been a real person," I asked, "I could have killed him?"

The mere question made them take another step back. I looked around. Other people, who probably saw what I had done to the mayor, started gathering and whispering at a safe distance.

"Not that I want to kill anyone, of course," I assured them. "It's just interesting to know. Has anyone ever died here before?"

I remembered what the pale woman had said, that you couldn't die in Heaven. But I couldn't be sure. Everything seemed more and more surreal. Waking up in Heaven, visiting the Plain of Souls, the entrance to the city, the fact I had no idea who I was or what I was doing there - all these made me start thinking, again, that maybe I was dreaming all this. Maybe I was lying, crushed, at the side of some road? And even if I wasn't and Heaven wasn't this trippy, perhaps the pale woman had been a dream? Or at least some sort of AI?

"We've never heard of anyone dying here," Jackie said quietly.

"No. It's never happened."

The Johnsons stood with their backs to the city, frozen in place. But behind them activity was stirring. Over the building an odd static hum started to rise, growing louder. The invisible energy dome I had crashed into changed its appearance. At first it had been completely transparent, but now it started to reflect the pink mountains, the clouds, the rainbow, and the blue sky.

A number of people noticed this change and pointed toward the city. After them a few more, and then, everyone. Jackie and José turned around and watched.

The humming got stronger and louder, until it became deafening.

And then they came out of the dome. Thousands of yellow-and-black dots, rapidly approaching us. My first thought was that they were wasps. Thousands of giant wasps, each one the size of my fist, with a vicious stinger and two yellow glowing eyes, focused only on me.

"Royal, I don't think you should stay -" I heard Jackie say.

I beamed far away from there.

From a mile away the city looked smaller and the humming sounded weaker. But then at once it grew louder. A black-and-yellow cloud manifested in the air eighty feet behind me. I didn't hesitate for a moment and beamed again, another mile forward. Then again. Then again. And then again.

I looked back. I was close to one of the mountaintops overlooking the valley. The city stood there glistening in the middle of the lake, small and distant. The humming had stopped.

And then it came back, weaker, a few hundred feet away from me. I took a deep breath and beamed again. This time I wasn't going to experiment and wait. I looked straight forward and started a series of beams, one after the other.

The scenery around me changed quickly. The green valley gave way to a chain of majestic mountains, the warm air changed into biting coldness, the rustic scenery changed to snow and ice. And still I beamed onward. I beamed over the highest mountain and then I stopped. This time I didn't look back. On the contrary. I looked straight forward, three hundred miles away, to the top of another mountain. A lower one.

Three hundred miles.

I took a deep breath, focusing on the top, and beamed forward.

I didn't expect to make it. The limit was one mile. I shouldn't be able beam farther. And even if I did succeed, I was sure it would take a little longer to get there.

I was surprised. Not only did I succeed, but it was easy. And the transit time continued to be immediate, with no relation to the distance traveled. For a moment I felt butterflies in my stomach, and then a different sensation. Warmer. I laughed out loud.

*

-"I'd laugh, too."
- "Yeah. It just felt right, breaking the rules. Being different. So I couldn't go into the cities in Heaven? So what? There would be a way around that. But if everyone could only beam a mile at a time and I could go farther... that was very interesting."

*

I landed in a mountainous area, only not quite so cold. The snow was melting slowly over black, granite rocks, the sound of dripping water came from every crevice. A gentle breeze whistled from within the rocks and a flock of green birds circled around the valley, not far from me. There was no sign or hum of the wasps. I was sure I had lost them along the way. In any case, I now knew I could evade them easily, if and when they finally found me. I calmed down.

I wasn't ready for the sabertooth tiger's attack.

It started as a giant tooth coming out of my chest, lifting me like a crane and shaking me from side to side, tearing me from within.

At this point I felt no pain, only surprise. I understood I was in the jaws of something, and I remembered the creatures I had seen underwater in the lake around Midlake.

In the meantime, the tiger's jaw clamped down on me from

55

behind, and then came the pain. Harsh, paralyzing. I tried to grab on to something with my hands, kick with my legs, but there was nothing I could do. Except one thing.

I beamed forward. Not much. Not more than twenty feet. But that was enough. It was almost funny seeing the giant cat with nothing but air in his mouth, while I, his prey, was plastered to a rock, shooting jets of bright blood everywhere.

It roared and charged again. Four hundred and forty pounds of a nightmare, extinct from the world for some ten thousand years, resurrected here in Heaven, with fangs a foot long. The first leap brought him about ten feet away from me. His second leap introduced him to my fist.

*

-*"The mighty fist strikes again."*
-*"Precisely."*
-*"How did you know it would work?"*
-*"Desperation? Gamer's instinct? Anyway, it worked. I punched the nose of an angry, ten-foot-long sabertooth tiger. Not a lot of people can say that."*

*

The fist went straight into the giant cat and it turned into gray fragments of dust. Just like the mayor before it. The gray cloud drifted slowly down to the ground, painted by the dark jets of blood still coming out of my body. The cliffs around me continued to echo the tiger's roar.

I was seriously wounded. And very tired.

I tried to stop the bleeding from my chest with my hand. I couldn't. The bite had come through my back, and there was no way I could reach the entrance wound. I could only lean on one of the rocks and ponder, once again, what the pale woman had told me about death in Heaven. I was about to find out if it was even possible. And anyway, if Heaven's system didn't recognize me, what exactly would happen? Would I become gray dust like the AI?

Perhaps I would just end and vanish.

And then... then I came up with a new idea. Perhaps the mayor was right? Perhaps I was an AI that had somehow grown a personality and become real? The Pedia was feeding my mind old and irrelevant information about Kurzweil's singularity, but I wasn't in the mood to dwell on the subject. I was dying and the pain was undoubtedly real.

The blood loss was real too, judging by the wave of weakness crawling through my body.

To my right came a loud chirp. I glanced around briefly. One of the green birds had landed a few feet away from me was examining me through yellow eyes. It chirped again and opened its sharp beak, which contained a row of even sharper teeth. A long tongue flicked across them and the beak snapped shut.

Another bird landed next to it, then another. The pace of their beaks snapping grew in rhythm and strength. Above me, more green birds started circling, surrounding me. I felt trapped. I was ready to accept being bitten to death by a sabertooth tiger, but not being pecked to death by a flock of birds with sharp beaks. I felt around on the ground with my free hand until I found a stone big enough. I threw it at the first bird I saw. In actuality, I didn't throw it. It was more like a shot. The stone shot out of my hand and turned the bird into a gray dust cloud.

The other birds didn't react at all. Perhaps they were happy one of their competitors was out of the picture, leaving a bigger portion for the rest. They started approaching me with little bounces. I started throwing rocks faster and faster and, one after another, they turned into dust.

I was quickly running out of stones, but more importantly, I was running out of time. My vision was becoming blurry and the jets of blood shooting out of me had slowed and turned into a slow seep. I guessed I didn't have a lot of blood left. Still, I was pretty sure I could destroy every bird that came near me. As long as I could stay conscious. As long as I was not too tired to fight.

And then I heard it again. The humming.

Within seconds they were upon me. Hundreds of wasps coming from all directions, jamming hundreds of painful pitchforks into me.

Up close I saw that they weren't exactly wasps. Although they had black-and-yellow bodies, their form was human – female - aside from their transparent wings. Like fairies. Angry fairies. I managed to squash a few, but the rest kept stabbing me with more and more little pitchforks, each one of them no bigger than a toothpick, but very painful.

My vision flickered a few times and then went dark.

MEMORY 3

The mist came, the mist went away.

I was in another world. Not the world I was living in. It was a colorful world, scarier, more exciting. I tried to remember its name. I couldn't, even though I knew it. I was frustrated by it.

I was the king of my kingdom, ordering my seconds-in-command to draft soldiers for me. I had a purpose. I had a mission. I looked at the horizon, at another kingdom. I hated it so much, I hated its king. He kept sending his workers to my borders and constantly stole my wealth and power. He assassinated my children; he threatened to conquer my kingdom and destroy me. And now, I knew, he was recruiting a massive army, about to invade my land.

But I saw it coming. I waited for him. I led my soldiers to the border and waited.

Dust rose in the distance and I knew he was on his way to crush me. I also knew he could. His kingdom was bigger and richer. I couldn't handle an attack head-on, face-to-face. But I had no plans to do that. I wanted to let him pass me by, to just go on, as if it was nothing. I would dig into the ground and wait. Not long. Soon his troops approached the border. He had blue and green dragons, he had armored vehicles, he had agile salamanders, and he had planes I couldn't reach.

They all passed me by, all stepped on the ground a few inches above my troops, who were hiding in the trenches. For a moment I fought the urge to break out from below and try to surprise him. But I wasn't so sure I would win, even if I did manage to surprise his troops. Instead, I waited patiently. Swallowed the insult. Waited.

The last of his soldiers went past us and disappeared over the hill. Quietly, I climbed out of the ground and charged into his kingdom. With all my strength and speed. Speed was most important. Because of it, I had to sacrifice a large number of my troops. I wanted to charge his palace quickly. He, on the other end, had already spotted me. He called his army back, to withdraw from my land and come back home, hoping to cut me off and trap me in the middle.

I took the gamble and kept on charging. I had an agile cavalry and wild, explosive geese. A light force, very light. Not many would do what I did, but I knew I was doing the right thing. One after the other, his posts collapsed. They couldn't hold me back for long, but they cost me many soldiers. I was excited. It was all or nothing.

Suddenly, I was in his palace. I closed the gates to his troops and everyone was left outside; before me was only one king, alone, defenseless, and with no way out. I got off my horse and slew him where he stood.

Happiness. Pleasure. Power. All his troops became mine. And I should have been happy, but I wasn't. I felt sad and empty. I had won the game, but I knew something bad was about to happen.

The mist came, the mist went away.

DEATH

Again the white light. And again this horrible pain. Only this time it was on a lower scale. Less bright, less deafening. Still an unpleasant experience, but not so awful. Perhaps I had grown accustomed to it?

"To be honest, I expected you to be back here a lot faster," I heard a familiar voice say.

I gurgled a little in response. It was the white angel. Turns out she was right: you really don't die here, in Heaven. Not for long, at least. I wondered if, somewhere, there was a counter, counting how many times you got killed. If it meant anything.

"Don't exhaust yourself. Your voice will come back shortly. It's not like the first time, when you had to be put together from scratch. Here, look, even your body's ready."

I looked. It really was there. Black and strong and wonderful, a complete and lovely opposite to the pure, marble shade of her skin. And the redness of her lips. It was exactly the same shade as the pasties she wore; this time they were shaped like hearts.

I wondered if she had a matching set in the form of Hello Kitty.

"What are you doing here?"

She smiled and came near me without a word. I found I was no longer tired.

*

-"I figured she'd be back. It's her job, apparently."

-"That's what I thought, but just then, I didn't care. After all I'd been through, I thought I deserved a few moments of happiness. But like everything good, it also went away."

*

"Why… why did you think I'd be back here?"

"Because you'd miss me, of course."

I couldn't help smiling.

"Where did you disappear to last time?"

"I had to go. The… boss needed me."

60

I relaxed for a moment. Then, with a swift and determined movement, I got up off the bed and searched for my black robe. It was on the floor, wrinkled, but a light shake brought it back to its shiny, perfect state. I walked toward the door with a steady face, not looking back.

Turns out I didn't need to look back. In a split second she appeared before me and blocked my way. Her indigo eyes drilled into mine.

"Where do you think you're going?"

"To a place where I won't be lied to."

She nodded her head lightly and something changed in her gaze.

"I see. Sit."

She moved out of my way so I could get out of the room unhindered, if I chose to.

I didn't choose to. I went back to the edge of the bed and sat down. She sat down beside me.

"What would you like to know?"

"What I've always wanted to know. Who am I?"

"I can't tell you that."

"Can't, or won't?"

She hesitated. "Ask me something else," she eventually said.

There was no point. I got up and started walking toward the exit.

This time, she didn't bother blocking my way. "You can't really get out of here, you know."

"Great," I said. "If you'd like to talk to me, you know where to find me."

I walked through the door.

*

-"I would have stayed there, to find out."

-"Perhaps. But I couldn't stick around for a moment longer. I was sick of everything."

-"How typical - get up and run away."

-"Honestly, I thought I wouldn't make it. I thought the door would be blocked by the same kind of shield that covered Midlake. So when I went up to it, I extended my hands forward first. But nothing stopped them. Nothing stopped me, either."

*

Heaven was scented and wonderful, just as I remembered. The colors were wonderful in that same way as well. I closed my eyes, took a deep breath, and listened to the silence. The peace.

The distant humming ruined it. A familiar humming.

My heart skipped a beat. Why were they here? How did they know I was here? I panicked and tried to beam away. But I couldn't really go far. The trees were too close together and all I could do was move a few feet at a time. After the fifth time, I got a better idea: to climb to the top of a tree and beam away from there, as far as possible. But it was too late.

The strange fairies swooped in on me from all directions and turned out the lights.

*

A bright light. Harsh pain. Massive noise from everywhere. And anger. Lots of anger.

"I'm sorry," I heard her say from a distance. "This time it will take you longer to wake up. If you die too quickly, the system punishes you."

Even if I had wanted to say something to her at that point, I couldn't speak.

"I told you the truth. You can't get out of here," she said, almost apologetically.

I tried to turn my head and look at her, but I didn't have a head to turn just yet. In any case, the noise was too painful.

*

-*"Let me guess: you lost consciousness."*
-*"Exactly."*

*

When I opened my eyes again, I already had a body, I had a head, and I had a headache. My vision hadn't yet adjusted to the white brightness of the room, and I still heard suspicious ringing, but I ignored all that. I sat up in bed, dazed. A few seconds later she came into the room and closed the door.

"Better?"

62

"Better," I answered. "How did you know this would happen?"

"The system tagged you as a threat. Anywhere your digital signature appears, it will activate a defense. So it's true, you cannot die in Heaven. But making sure you never leave this place is certainly possible."

Suddenly the white walls seemed a lot more threatening. "Are there... are there other people like me here? That the system won't let out?"

Silently, she nodded her head.

I realized I had a serious problem. I started planning my escape immediately. I already knew the first step: as soon as I got out of here, I would have to climb to the top of one of the trees and from there start beaming forward. But what then? Constantly running? The system was everywhere; it would track me down no matter where I went. I couldn't elude it, and I couldn't even get out of it. I was, myself, part of the system! And I didn't even know who I was.

That was apparently the key to all my problems. I needed to find out who I was and why the system didn't recognize me. But first I needed to know more about what waited for me in the first stage of my escape.

"Those things that attacked me that look like little angry fairies. What are those?"

She sat on the bed next to me, thigh almost touching thigh. "Those are the terror pixels. No one likes them here. They're like the immune system of the system."

She placed a hand on my thigh, stroking it, and then started sliding it upward. I didn't like it. Although I did like it. I barely managed to move her hand off me, placing it back on her thigh. This wasn't the time for that. My body was still sore, my head hurt, and besides, I had to remind myself, I was mad at her.

"So now," I continued, not to be sidetracked from my investigation, "I can't leave this place?"

"Don't worry. We'll leave together. If there's one thing the pixels hate more than you, it's me. We'll leave together, and they'll come after me."

"And what about you?"

"I know how to handle them."

"How do you know that?"

"That's easy. I'm the one who programmed them."

*

-"What?"

-"That's exactly what I thought. But then I looked at her again, her perfect face and body, and deep down, I knew it was true. She was much more than I'd thought she was."

*

"Okay. Who are you?"

I should have asked that question long ago. Why hadn't I? Because I thought she wouldn't answer. Just like she hadn't answered any of my important questions so far. But she did answer me, in a way.

"You can call me Queen M. Or M, for short."

"And I know you from my previous life?"

M laughed. "I'd find that hard to believe."

"And you were the one who programed the terror pixies?"

"Terror pixels. But yeah, now that you've said it, perhaps 'pixies' is more suitable."

"So you are actually part of the system?"

M frowned, disgusted.

"I most certainly am not. Maybe I used to be, a long time ago. But now, they don't really like me here. And I don't like them either."

"Why?"

"Because they love to rule. To take ownership of all the information, all the details, all the power. And I think that in Heaven, it should be different. No one should control anyone else."

"What do you mean, control?"

"Look at you. You're trapped in here instead of walking around outside, for no reason. You've committed no crime."

"Of course I didn't! Wait, can you commit a crime here? What's considered a crime?"

"Nothing!" She got up off the bed. "There are no crimes here! So why are they hurting you?"

I couldn't agree more. What did I want? To know who I was? To get into the city? I couldn't understand why I couldn't go into the city and understood even less how they could think I was an AI. Why would evil pixies chase me? Why lock me in here? If there was a system causing all that, something about it was seriously wrong.

"I have a question," I said. "If they don't like you, why aren't they

64

hurting you, like they're hurting me?"

"I'm not that easy to hurt," she whispered in my ear. Then she placed her hand back on my thigh.

This time I didn't push her away. I hugged her gently and we clung to each other. Her lips found their way to mine and I pushed all thought aside. All but one rebellious thought: control can be gained through suffering, but also through pleasure. Even more effectively.

*

-*"You're so easy."*
-*"I know. And undoubtedly was a lot more so afterwards. When there are things that make you get such a stupid grin on your face, why not give in to them?"*

*

The hours passed. I don't know how many.

Eventually, we started getting ready to venture out. She reattached her red heart pasties, I put on my robe, and we both faced the exit. I was a little hesitant about going through it. The last memory I had of the terror pixies was still fresh in my mind. But M promised it was going to be fine.

She had a plan.

"I have an idea about how you can find out who you are," she said.

"How? Where?"

She hesitated. "It won't be simple. You have to get far away, to a place that's not so... friendly. You won't like it."

My eyes lit up. At that moment, there was nothing I wouldn't do to know more about my identity and about my past downstairs. I was ready to risk anything. What could happen? I'd die? Then I'd find myself back here again. And start over. I convinced her to tell me what I needed to do.

"Once we leave here, the pixies will come. I'll draw them to me," she explained. "And you'll have to start beaming toward the ocean. You remember where that is?"

I nodded. I thought that downstairs, I might not have had much of a sense of direction, but here in Heaven, everything was clearer.

On one side were mountains, the other side the sea. I knew where to beam to.

"It will take you at least a hundred beams to get to the beach," she continued. For a moment I thought of updating her on my newfound ability, but decided against it. "Some of the pixies will continue coming after you, so don't stop beaming. When you reach the beach, turn right and keep beaming. Your goal is to reach the place where the rainbow touches the ground. That's in the jungle."

She hesitated a moment and then went on. "It's not an ordinary jungle. You'll need a bit of courage to get through it. Try to do it as quickly as possible. Don't listen to anything around you, don't talk to anyone, and don't try to investigate anything. Just try to reach the rainbow as fast as you can."

"What's there? Monsters?"

"It doesn't really matter. No one goes there anyway. It's just an obstacle you need to get past. You think you can do it?"

With one beam, I thought to myself. With one beam I could do it.

"I think you can do it, too. When you reach the rainbow, you'll find a pool. I'll meet you there."

"What about the pixies?"

"If you beam fast enough, you'll lose them. Even if you run into new ones, you just have to stay as far away from them and move as fast as possible."

"Okay," I said, "but I have one condition."

She looked at me with those indigo eyes of hers. "Don't worry. If you make it to the pool, you'll know who you really are."

"And if I don't?"

She smiled. "Come on, let's get out of here."

ESCAPE

We walked out of the door hand in hand. It was my idea, to hold her - so she couldn't disappear on me like the last time. She didn't resist, and as we went through the door, I thought how silly it really was. I was still a captive of the downstairs way of thinking. That 'holding' meant really holding on to someone, physically.

But her hand felt nice. It gave me a sense of security. So we held hands and I closed my eyes.

I stepped forward. A sweet, fragrant wind blew on my face and pleasant sounds came to my ears. I was back in the green forest and this time I wasn't alone. I looked at M admiringly. Until that moment, I had only seen her against the white background of the awakening rooms. But here, against the lush green background of the trees, the stunning blue of the sky, and the yellow, red, orange, and purple of the flowers - she was completely different. A radiant white angel. Here in a world where colors had real meaning, her absolute paleness created an exceptionally dramatic presence. Much like my total black, I supposed.

Within seconds the forest was filled with the familiar humming. A large swarm of pixies came out of the trees and flew straight at us.

"Go!" M pushed me and then beamed twenty feet away. She gestured something to the pixies with her hands and they changed course and swooped at her.

Despite wanting to get as far away as fast as possible, I lingered to look at the scene for a few more seconds. It was very peculiar. The pixies covered her quickly, but they seemed to go through her. They tried to stab her, but it was like stabbing air. The swarm just went through her over and over and over again.

"What are you waiting for? Beam out of here!"

I beamed.

*

-"How many beams did it take you to reach the sea?"
-"Four beams, each one about thirty miles."
-"And how was it?"

67

-"I was starting to enjoy it. Control it. In fact, for the first time since I arrived in Heaven, I didn't feel lost. I had a purpose, I had a calling. Maybe I was being chased, but I had a good feeling."

*

I tried to see where the big rainbow crossing the sky met the ground. It looked like that spot was on the other side of the world. A thousand miles away from me. Perhaps even tens of thousands. A long way.

The last beam brought me to the beach, although the ocean didn't look like any ocean that existed downstairs. I felt it just before taking the last beam, far away from the beach. I could hear the gentle sound of the waves from there, and for a moment I wondered what kind of waves could be heard from such a height. But I was busy concentrating on running away from the pixies chasing me and on the last beam, which I aimed at a lone cliff protruding from the sand, watching over the waves.

Distance can be deceiving. That little cliff was two miles high, give or take. The waves crashing against it were hundreds of feet tall. From afar, the sound was a murmur. Up close, it was like a fleet of old Boeing 7127s all taking off at once. I had trouble hearing my own thoughts.

So I stood there, at the top of the cliff, and watched a monstrous wave forming slowly about ten miles off the beach. Slowly it lifted over the ocean, like Poseidon rising from his slumber, gaining momentum as it grew. With endless patience, it built up speed, and as it did, I noticed it picked up a little debris on its bow. Little light specks riding the top of the wave.

Debris, was it?

I farscoped to the front of the wave, where like kings of the world, a few people surfed, each one on their board, getting ready for the moment that the mega-wave would reach its peak and break. They looked like California surfers from the previous century: deep bronze tans, wavy blond hair, eyes narrowed in concentration, and smiles filled with pure pleasure. Even though everything looked like it was moving in slow motion, I knew they were moving at a speed of over sixty miles an hour, and that it was only the beginning.

My heart pinched. I was jealous of them.

The noise grew louder and the wave finally broke. White foam started forming at its top and the group of surfers made their way down the waves, leaving it way above them, cutting white paths over the wall of water. The beach got closer and closer and the oceanic titan matured into the perfect wave, classic. Its upper part started falling down and forward, bigger and stronger than Niagara Falls, while it created the perfect surfing tunnel, thousands of gallons of water.

You couldn't die in Heaven, I reminded myself. But you sure could have fun here.

And then it came. As the wave folded into itself, less than a mile from the beach, the surfers started surfing out of it, one after the other, at nearly one hundred and twenty miles an hour. They came from the side closest to me, fighting the sweeping headwind, aiming themselves into the little lagoon by the side of the mountain.

The mountain! At the last moment I realized what the mountain's true purpose was. I looked around me. Even two miles above the surface, it was filled with fresh puddles of seawater that hadn't had a chance to evaporate or be absorbed by the ground. Suddenly I realized how it had gotten this far. The noise became unbearable, the white wall of water rapidly came closer, and at the last second, before it crashed into the mountain with a might that could put me back in the white room, I beamed away from it to the only place I could see at that moment.

*

-*"The end of the rainbow?"*
-*"I wish I had done that. But no. I wanted to be with those surfers so badly that I stayed. I knew it wasn't the right time, but still, I had to talk to them."*

*

The lagoon at the foot of the mountain was perfect. Still, smooth water, deep turquoise shade, existing as a complete contradiction to the wave's arena right next to it. In the water there were a few sun loungers, a few people resting on them, cans of Carlsberg in their hands. Calm, ambient music came from a hidden source and some of the people moved to its rhythm. Behind me, on the white, clean beach, stood a professional barbecue station, and from it came the intoxicating scent of roasted meat. The surfers I had watched earlier huddled next to it, picking out prime bits for themselves.

I was the only one there who was dressed.

One of the surfers noticed me and, with a full mouth, signaled me to come closer. He was almost as tall as I was, very tanned, with long bronze hair down to the middle of his back. He had eyes the color of eggplant and strawberry lips.

"Duke." He extended his hand toward me, offering a juicy T-bone steak. I sank my teeth into it and was transported to a world of a different kind of pleasure.

"God..." I could only moan, when I was able to open my mouth again.

Duke smiled with a full mouth.

"Royal, I mean. My name is Royal. God is probably the one who put this steak on the grill."

"You must mean Rage," Duke said, and pointed to one of the surfers. He was a living statue of muscles, with skin the shade of lightning and eyes of flame. Literally, flames. He stood just outside the pack and looked at the water. "Closest thing to God here."

*

-*"Trash."*
-*"Exactly. And I didn't know, at the time, who he was."*
-*"You're an idiot."*
-*"Don't push it. I didn't go to him directly. Just the opposite, in fact."*

*

I took another bite of steak. "That was quite a wave you surfed."

"Quite a wave, indeed. You should try it too. Were you a surfer, downstairs?"

"Not waves this big," I replied vaguely. "Are you here a lot?"

"Sometimes when we get off the needle. Usually, it's all up to Rage."

"The needle?" I wondered out loud.

Duke chuckled, half apologetic. "I know, I know. We're from the needle. Now complain we're snobs."

"I'm not complaining at all," I said, smiling.

"Nonsense. Feel free. It's your fault you asked about it... you must be new here, right?"

70

"True. Only a few days."

Duke's eyes widened with curiosity, then narrowed with slight concern. He glanced at Rage. The closest thing to God was busy devouring a steak the size of a cat and talking to a couple of girls. Duke seemed to relax, and placed a hand on my waist and guided me gently to the other side of the lagoon.

"Tell me," he whispered, "is there any news? What's the situation down there?"

I tried to avoid a straight answer. "Why do you ask?"

He glanced at Rage again and then to some of his companions. "I lost touch with my son a few weeks ago. He used to tell me the news regularly, but now he's not answering." He smiled apologetically. "I'm a little worried."

"I completely understand. How old is he, your son?"

"Seventy-eight. You'll meet him, I saved him a spot here. But now I can't find him. Or his family. It's driving me crazy!"

"Where does he live?"

"Boulder, Colorado. He works in the system's complex. Maintenance."

*

-"Boulder, Colorado?"
-"Exactly."

*

I didn't want to be the one to give him the news. Surely not when the closest thing to God was there, right next to us, eating a steak, which he probably seared himself, with his eyes. But I was in a catch-22. I remembered what the Johnsons had told me: thought is speech. Speaking is thinking. I couldn't think 'out loud' about what I didn't want to tell him. He'd pick up on it. So I focused on the ocean, imagining the big wave crashing against the mountain again.

I couldn't lie to him completely either. So I chose to repeat what I already knew.

"The world, downstairs? Rotting slowly." I repeated what I had heard at the Plain of Souls. "Between the Caliphate here and the Newborn there."

"The Caliphate are not a concern to me. They can have Europe,

71

but if they think of crossing the ocean, we'll annihilate them. But the Newborn... they are a problem. Especially since you never know who they are. Anyone could suddenly turn on you!"

I nodded my head, concentrating on the crashing wave. "Yeah, you're right."

"Even here, we've caught some Newborn."

My ears perked up. "What? What did you do with the ones you caught?"

"We neutralized them. Rage has his methods."

My head wanted to race in directions it shouldn't go, and I tried, forcefully, to concentrate harder on the breaking wave. I imagined myself surfing it. I imagined myself diving into it. I imagined M diving in it. I pictured the rushing water... wave, wave, wave. Blue, big, wild, raging. I had to think of nothing but the wave. The next wave. And the next wave.

"I see you're waiting for another wave." Duke smiled and patted my back. "Go, enjoy. Maybe we'll join you later."

He went toward the food and I was left alone.

I looked at the group of people having fun on this perfect beach. I inhaled the scent of perfect steaks and heard the fizzing of the beer in the glasses, which I had no doubt was perfect too. I wanted to be a part of that perfection. This calmness.

Then suddenly, I wanted the opposite. To just leave that place, disappear, get out, and follow the rainbow.

But first, I had to go somewhere else.

GLIMPSE

Of course I didn't go surfing.

But I also didn't come close to the end of the rainbow. It could wait. Instead, I went back to the Plain of Souls. I had to find out more about myself, and discover it myself. Without any help. Not even M's.

The Plain of Souls was the only place I had a chance of retrieving that information. True, it was very far away, but that meant nothing to me. I had already grown accustomed to my ability to beam longer distances in the blink of an eye. It's amazing how fast you get used to good things. It was already a part of me. How could anyone get by without it?

The scenery around me changed twice, and the third time I was there, under a gloomy sky, walking on ancient, desert soil, with the distant thunder echoing in my ears. Around me were a lot of white souls, each one concentrating on their own well. There were a lot more, substantially more than when I had come here with José and Jackie. I wondered what the reason might be.

I didn't like being in the crowd. I wanted a secluded well, without anyone passing by or looking in on what I was searching for. After a few short beams, I found one.

Just like the first well I visited, this one was not anything more than a crude circle in the sand, marked by red bricks and in its center a dark hole. When I had come here before, Jackie and José had activated it. Now I was alone. And nothing happened.

I waved my hands over the well. Nothing.

I called into it. "Hello? Anybody? Yo!"

Silence.

I looked around to see if anyone was coming near me or sensed I was acting weird. But all the souls were still far away from me. No one came near me and I didn't hear any pixies swarming around. They hadn't followed me to the beach either, I remembered. Maybe M didn't know everything about the system. The other people I saw were far away, each one focused on their own well, lit from below, probably fully invested in a conversation with a son, a grandson, or a spouse.

And maybe that was the whole point?

Maybe I couldn't activate the well because I just didn't have a specific person to contact. I didn't know anyone downstairs. How could I? I didn't even know myself. I realized this, too, could be a simple problem of identification. The system couldn't identify me, so the well wouldn't work. I was blocked out of the Plain of Souls. Just like the cities.

And then a pulse of fear surged through me. Would the system be able to identify someone trying to activate it? Someone unknown? For a moment I expected a swarm of pixies to pounce on me again. But no humming came from the horizon. Only vague, threatening rolls of thunder. I was safe. For a few moments, at least.

I looked at the well in frustration. I'd had high hopes for it. I wanted to find out what had happened downstairs so badly, to try and figure out who was looking for me. It was obvious to me someone must be looking for me. Certainly, I had some descendent waiting anxiously for me to make contact.

And maybe, I suddenly thought, maybe I was one of those killed during the attack from the Newborn? The timing was right. Trash, I could have been Duke's son! Maybe they had tried to save my life and had uploaded me into the system without proper preparation? And because of the emergency, I came up to Heaven without my memory. That option seemed very realistic to me. I struggled against the urge to go back to the beach and turn to Duke directly.

But it was foolish. I couldn't risk myself like that. Somewhere, I was sure, someone was looking for me. I had to find them. I had to know what was going on downstairs. To know what the news -

The well lit up.

*

-"*And where did you get to? Home?*"

*

The well connected, but not to a house or a specific person.

On the contrary, there wasn't anything personal at all. Instead, I got exactly what I had been thinking about: a news review on what was happening in the world.

I can't even describe my disappointment. But still, the news was very interesting.

It started, of course, with the European Jihad. The fortification of London, the Palace of Versailles going up in flames, beheadings in Spain, the Acropolis wiped out, the mosques spreading, the green and black colors taking over the old continent. Bitter battles raged outside Berlin. Switzerland still existed, but for how long? The news couldn't predict.

Afterward, the East Asia review. The Chinese Empire, the third Korean War, a glimpse of Russia, the isolationist. And then the technology section, focusing this time on smart implants and an in-depth review of the groundbreaking breakthrough in quantum computerization. It turned out that a new generation was being developed, managing to control more variations of the universe, and it could be implemented in Heaven within a year.

That was where they debated the different interpretations. Three experts argued in the studio about the question of whether Heaven would be open to absorbing more people, or if it was just an improvement of the current conditions. That was when it got heated. On one side was a gray-haired man who claimed that the social differences Heaven created were tearing America apart, and a colorful young woman claimed the technology was expensive and therefore available only to those who could afford it and that was how it should be.

I walked away from the well, a jumble of thought.

The well darkened.

I left.

MEMORY 4

The mist came, the mist went away.

She was as beautiful as the horizon, thrilling like a storm in summertime. Even her name was exciting; I couldn't stop saying it in my heart. And it was weird, because when I tried remembering it, I couldn't.

The truth is, she wasn't as beautiful as the horizon. My friends didn't think she was anything special at all. But I knew differently. She was the most special thing I had ever seen. She had lovely freckles under two laughing eyes, and a thin mouth that rounded occasionally with wonder. And I loved her. I loved her so much.

Even when she had braces on her teeth, I loved her. She was just as special. Just as attractive. When the braces came off, and those pearly whites shone out of her mouth uninterrupted, I didn't love her more— I just felt I was right to have loved her before.

She loved wearing pink sweaters, and I imitated her and bought a pink umbrella. In the winter, at the height of a rainstorm, when we all got stuck inside the school cafeteria, I gave her the umbrella so she could get to her class. She returned it to me the next day with a polite thank you. I was sure she'd leave me a message on the umbrella, something written, perhaps her address. But no, the umbrella came back just as it had been, with no way to communicate with her.

And at recess, on the stairs, I tried talking to her. But I lost my head and the only thing that came out were a few weak words while she passed by me with her friends. I held on to the rail desperately so as not to fall. I loved her so much and she didn't love me back. And I hated her for it.

But I still loved her.

The mist came, the mist went away.

RAINBOW

I started beaming my way back. The beach went on for hundreds of miles and I traversed it easily. I was emotionally drained. Downstairs, the Earth was falling apart, and I still didn't know who I was and why I was like this. The only solution I could think of was on the other side of Heaven, where an imaginary rainbow met virtual land. Trash.

I didn't stay put for more than a few seconds, trying to absorb as little information along the way as I could. Keep as much of my energy as possible. When I had woken up in the white room, I was completely refreshed, but I knew it was only a matter of time until the experiences started piling up and I would start yawning again. At some point, I would need to enter one of the sleeping cities to unload. I didn't know how I was going to do that.

I went distractedly through a tropical area with tall palm trees full of huge coconuts spreading out over white sandy beaches. I had no doubt the coconuts would taste extraordinary, but I did not have time to find out. I beamed onward.

*

I was in a watery swamp that reeked with the harsh scent of sulfur. To my left, above the foam of the water, rose the giant head of a water lizard. Its eyes were red and round. They focused on me and it opened its massive mouth, filled with sharp teeth, and rapidly approached me. The giant head was at the end of an amazingly long neck, several feet long. I beamed onward.

*

I was on a colorful strip of beach that wasn't made of sand, but of insanely colored pebbles, and above them a layer of soap bubbles as high as my shoulder. I made my way through the bubbles, enjoying the vortex of pleasant sensation all over my body. I wanted to stay there forever and never worry about anything ever again. I gritted my teeth and beamed onward.

*

I was in a dark place, with phosphorescent naked bodies laughing, bathing, and splashing water at one another. I beamed onward.

*

Rain washed over me from everywhere, strong winds whistled in my ears. To my left, out on the sea, a seventeenth century pirate ship battled the winds, with black sails and the Jolly Roger whipping fiercely. I beamed onward. And I beamed onward. And I beamed onward. I started to get tired. And began to worry. Memories started to grip me, slow me down, and drag me back. As much as I wanted to forget, to be free, they jammed hungrier teeth into me.

And all of them were new memories. The kind I didn't want. The kind I wasn't looking for. I started dragging my legs, breathing heavily, and still I beamed further more and more, with my eyes slowly closing. Another cliff, another valley, another flock of seagulls, some more dog-sized crabs, more violins in the wind, more beautiful people walking around, more sensations, more memories slowing me down, more and more.

*

-"*How long did you keep going?*"
-"*A long time. But eventually I fell to my knees, tired as I had never been before. Agonizing exhaustion, painful. Because inside of me, I knew that if I so much as placed my head on the sand and closed my eyes, I'd fall asleep. That wouldn't help me. I could only get real rest in a sleeping city.*"
-"*Did you reach such a city?*"
-"*No. But I got somewhere else.*"

*

I looked up and I saw it. A huge rainbow, monumental, coming out of the clouds, painting the sky with the red, orange, yellow, green, and purple, and meeting the ground at such a distant spot I almost laughed at the irony. Of course, I couldn't reach there. Unless... unless I could beam there in one straight shot.

Only I couldn't do it. I couldn't see the spot where the rainbow touched the ground. There were mountains and forests in the way, and the base of the rainbow was hidden far behind them. I closed my eyes; I tried to imagine the future. What would it be like, lying on a beach, utterly spent? Would I die slowly from hunger and thirst, only to wake up in the white room again? Or perhaps the pixies would come eventually and put me out of my misery?

I had the strength for maybe one final beam. I looked at the rainbow, at the spot I thought was a few miles above the land. I concentrated. And I beamed to it.

*

-*"All the way to the rainbow? How high was it?"*
-*"I don't know exactly, but it was obviously more than a couple of miles. Maybe hundreds of miles. Heaven is a very big place, and has very big things."*

*

I found myself close to the top of the rainbow. It was, undoubtedly, the highest place I had visited in Heaven. The rainbow emerged above me out of thick white clouds. I couldn't have seen through them even if I had had the energy or the desire. Instead, I looked down.

Heaven is not designed like a planet. It's not round. It is an endless surface, on which you can build anything. Two hundred and fifty miles away, I saw a range of white mountains that made the Himalayas look like an ant farm. Silver stripes, glistening in the sun, suggested massive twisting rivers. Vast green patches suggested extensive jungles, bordering dry yellow deserts. Occasionally, you could see traces of human construction: pyramids, towers, gigantic concrete cities, and other structures only possible in Heaven. Close to the ocean, a tall, narrow needle stuck out, reaching halfway up the rainbow's height. Next to it shimmered what could only be described as a perfect glass cube, the size of a mountain.

The current carried me. I was sliding down.

The rainbow in Heaven is not made of light. Well, it is, but that light is tangible. You can touch it. It flows. It lives. And it washed down at an incredible speed, rolling me slowly between the different rivers of color. The angle wasn't steep, but the flow of the colored rivers was very fast. Like a consistent dip in a river bed, allowing you to float in the water while it pulls you forward.

And I floated in it. Clouds went past me, some straight through me. The wind was pleasant, the colors all smelled wonderful. I wondered how many people had done this before, if anyone ever had. Probably not many. Few could beam as high as I had.

I discovered an additional fact: the light cured. The rainbow unloaded the load. The excess memories. Slowly, my exhaustion stopped burning. Stopped hurting. Turned into regular, drowsy, welcome fatigue.

I closed my eyes and allowed myself to doze off.

*

The first time I woke up because of a dream. More like a vision. I heard Jackie scream. Right next to me. I opened my eyes at once and looked right and left. She wasn't there. Just a massive, endless flow of calming and empowering colors. I thought I was hallucinating, ascribing it to the trauma I had gone through. I closed my eyes.

And I heard her again immediately. She squealed in pain, and this time a visual came with the sound. José was there. He was trapped between giant black jaws that looked like they belonged to a monstrous ant. It grabbed him from the top, biting an inch of his flesh and fur. Fresh blood slowly seeped out of the cuts. Lots of blood. José moaned in pain. His face was twisted.

"Let go of him!" I heard Jackie say, almost crying. I didn't see her, and suddenly I understood: I was seeing out of her eyes. I could see they were at Midlake's beach. "We know nothing about it!"

A number of pixies came into view. Their eyes looked deep into mine, as if they knew I could see out of her eyes. "Where did he hide the core code?" I heard a strong voice from an unknown source demand. I opened my eyes again.

The voices were gone. I kept on floating, helpless, in the flow of colors slowly sloping downward, high in Heaven's sky. I was tired and soon I fell asleep again.

*

The second time I woke up was because of a background noise that kept getting louder. It took me a few seconds to understand, to remember where I was and why. The wind was stronger, but it wasn't the source of the noise. The source of it was under me: an amazing waterfall, surrounded by a psychedelic, colorful, foamy cloud reaching hundreds of feet high. Although I was going downward, in a freefall, my speed had not changed. I was still a part of that river of light, flowing slowly toward the end of the rainbow.

I looked around; thick green jungle spread out forever, from one end of the horizon to the other. In the distance, I could see misty mountain tops. I couldn't decide which direction I had arrived from, or where the beach was. Even when I tried, it seemed like I just couldn't remember. The ground came closer, the noise grew louder. Naturally, I wanted to beam out of the rainbow, but then I stopped myself. My goal was to reach its end. The place where it met the ground and turned into... what?

And I wanted to feel it myself. I let the colorful light foam swallow me. I was ready for impact and I didn't close my eyes. At the last second I changed my position and dove headfirst. At the last second I smiled. You can't die in Heaven, I repeated to myself. You can't die!

The last thing I remembered, before impact, was that if you mix all the colors of the rainbow, you actually get white.

I started laughing uncontrollably.

A ROOM

It was a bad idea, laughing. It made me swallow some color.

It wasn't a bad feeling on its own—the rainbow's colors taste very good. The red color is like something between a watermelon and a cherry, an odd combination that has the stinging touch of first love, bitter, that makes it less sweet and more sensual. The orange was sort of like mango, but it also had the cool taste of a childhood summer vacation at the beach. The yellow resembled sugared sun rays, but behind them the depth of a bonfire-roasted corn on a romantic night. The blue had the taste of clear sky, speckled with caramel, coconut, and dulce de leche. The purple tasted like juicy, dripping honey, mixed with great horror films that leave your heart pounding with joy.

I stopped laughing and breathed. I opened my mouth, swallowed everything, and drowned in the blue pool.

All the other fragments of color disappeared. The world became blue and sweet and the massive waterfall of color pushed me downward so powerfully I couldn't even move aside. I waited for the moment I would reach the bottom of the pool, but that moment never came. Endless tons of blue color spilled over my head, pushing me further down. I reached a depth of almost two miles. My heart was pounding against my temples; the air in my lungs was running out.

I swam sideways, thinking the pressure would subside away from the main current. It didn't help. I kept diving down at the same speed, even when I reached the pool's vertical side wall. I found it was completely smooth, with nowhere to grip.

And then I saw it. A white, round opening, slightly below me, but further right, off of my diving route. I started swimming toward it wildly, but there was no chance I would get to it in time. The opening passed by me like a flash of light and almost disappeared in the deep blue accumulating above me. For a split second I was filled with despair, and then I remembered where I was and who I was.

At the last possible moment, I beamed to it.

*

-"What would have happened if you had missed?"

-"I really don't know. Maybe I would have come out Heaven's other side?"

-"What could be under Heaven?"

-"Good question. Maybe I would have just gone back to the top of the rainbow."

-"I doubt that. It's a virtual world. You don't really need to recycle the stream. Things can just..."

-"Disappear. Yeah."

*

I didn't disappear.

I was on all fours, panting wildly, at the opening of a long cave lit with a white, gleaming light. A few inches behind me, loud masses of liquid color kept falling into the unknown abyss. But inside the tunnel, as if in a bubble, the air was dry. And the silence absolute.

Not a sound from outside could be heard. At first I thought I heard a little undertone, but quickly I realized it was just the blood flowing through my body. The weak sounds of drumming echoing around me? My heartbeat, apparently.

I rose up and shook off out of instinct. But I had nothing to shake. Unlike water, the rainbow's color did not cling to my body or drip on the floor. It just stayed out of the tunnel, a blue, clear light.

I took a deep breath and walked forward with echoing footsteps. After several yards, the cave twisted and then climbed up at a slight gradient. It twisted again, straightened, and then ended abruptly. I was standing before a white wall on which two black handprints were stamped.

Exactly the size of my hands.

For a moment I hesitated, but I didn't see any other option. If I had reached this far, I had no reason to stop here. I pressed my palms to the wall and waited.

The memory melted into me like a sugar cube in hot water.

I was in my old room. I could see it. On the floor, in the back, was a pile of dirty laundry and on the bed was a clean pile. Mom, I remembered, had long ago given up on trying to put the laundry away in the closet. She realized the best way to make me change clothes was to just pick up the dirty ones from the floor and toss the clean ones on the bed. Which made the small room even smaller, with little room to move around.

But it didn't matter much. I didn't like to move anyway.

It was not the perfect memory. Not technically, and not depth-wise. Almost every neuro-movie is beautiful and more tangible than this was. But it was the first thing I remembered about myself, about my life downstairs. Despite it being bitter and sad, it was sweeter than any mango in Heaven.

*

-*"Big moment."*
-*"When you don't remember who you are, you live in total darkness. You don't know why you behave like you do. You don't know what to fear, what to love, what to hate. You feel things and don't know why. It's like being blind, or deaf."*
-*"Or dead."*

*

The mist came, the mist went away. And finally I had myself. Finally, I was Roy Shwartz, 204 pounds of shriveled fat, curly hair, troubled facial skin, and scary intelligence.

Most of it was still fuzzy. New memories surfaced in my consciousness like bubbles in a soda bottle. Sights. Sounds. Scents. Different times, different ages, different places. I remembered a red bicycle. I remembered soup and potatoes. Father's voice. Mother's soft hand. A computer. A broken heart. A broken hand. A grave. Blood. Crying. Rage.

And it was all jumbled together, all mixed up. There were a lot of lines to draw, to connect the dots. Lots of answers to unknown questions. But within a few minutes, more solid memories started to form. From the end to the beginning.

The last minute before I died and went to Heaven. The last hour. The last day. The last two weeks.

Those weeks, I remembered well. Especially the fear. Trash. Such fear.

MEMORY 5

The mist came, the mist went away.

The alarm went off exactly two weeks before I went up to Heaven.

They were probably at the bottom of the stairs, I guessed. Five minutes away from me, maybe ten minutes, maybe less. They were armed and they were coming to kill me. My heart was pounding. For a few days, I'd known I was in trouble and maybe - if I'd thought about what I was doing – I'd have made other decisions. But now it was too late. I had already hacked the system. I had already copied the core code. I had already made the stupid mistake that exposed me.

Dying at age seventeen. Trash. That was not what I thought would happen to me. It wasn't right.

I had always acted out of a sense of justice, I think. A sort of holy rage about everything that was messed up in the world. And there were a lot of messed up things in the world. The skies were no longer blue like in the old holos. The clouds were yellow, the hail was gray, and too many cities had slowly sunk into the sea, foundations crumbling.

You could see how messed up the world was from the news. The look in people's eyes - either moving in at an apathetic, drugged up crawl, or darting cunningly from side to side, like scavengers. You could find that out if you paid attention to the billions killed in Asia and Africa in the past decade, and the millions running away from the flames of Europe. You could read how messed up the world was in the new congressional laws closing the borders.

And, most of all, you could see it in the lengthening lines at the entrance to the system's Heaven, the same miraculous haven from the world, reserved only for those rich enough to get in before they died.

And I was angry. It shouldn't be like that. Heaven shouldn't only be reserved for the rich, or any other group. It should be open to everyone! And if it was a matter of money, well, everyone knew who had the money to finance its opening: the same ones who had closed it off to begin with. The ones who created it.

Someone had to open Heaven's doors.
And I decided that someone would be me.

*

Of course it wasn't easy. I invested over a year trying to hack the system; more than a year of sleepless nights, constant connection to the web, constant programming. They didn't skimp on firewalls, those guys, and I admired them for it. In addition, the whole interface was different from anything I knew. But I adapted.

Mother, God rest her soul, gave me all the freedom I needed. In my heart, I knew she was thinking about sending me to rehab. She was worried about me. She knew that if they found out about my previous hacks, it would ruin the way our little family had survived for the past few years. If I went to prison, she would lose her salary for many years to come. It was suicide. In a way, I turned myself into my own hostage, a technique I learned from the Caliphate.

Eventually, a month before it was all over, I managed to get into the system. One last firewall and I was in. I could see Heaven through my Neurox connection, and wandered around there like a ghost. I saw the people roaming around, what they did, and the way they behaved. I saw the giant waves, and I wanted to surf them. In reality, I could never go to the beach. But in Heaven? I could do anything.

I saw the areas that had already been built and those still under construction. I saw the rainbow, the needle, El-Paso, Valhalla, Tatooine... I saw, and was envious. So jealous. I wanted to be there. To build there. To live there.

From the outside, it looked like a game of Loom, but the difference was that it was real. In all the worlds I went to, in all other games, I always went back to being Roy Shwartz. The same lump of shapeless jelly that no girl wanted to come near, who lived in a crappy city with skies the color and taste of an ash storm, suicide bombings on the West Coast, artificial meat, and increasing global flooding. But I already knew: Heaven was real, it was tangible; when you reached it, you stayed in it forever.

*

I didn't know when exactly they found out I had hacked their system. But I wasn't the only one in the world who knew how to crack systems, and when you devote so much effort to attacking a monster like Heaven, naturally you cannot secure yourself from all sides.

I remembered it was the first time in my life that I actually felt fear. Perhaps the second time, if you count the moment when I had asked Miracle Green to meet me, a year before. I remembered my heart thumping before I asked her. I could barely see what was in front of me; black dots swam before my eyes and blocked my view. I was sweating and I'm pretty sure I stuttered. But I had to ask her. I had to know. And then she started avoiding me, with excuses, giggles—and suddenly she remembered she had a boyfriend. Two days before my sixteenth birthday. Some present she gave me.

It didn't stop her from asking things of me two days later. To run her errands. And I didn't mind giving her what she wanted. Part of me felt that if she had been here, asking me for things here too, I would still give them to her. Even though she never really loved me, and didn't really want me, because how can you love and want someone that looks like...

And I remembered, I didn't look like me anymore. I wasn't Roy Shwartz anymore. I was Royal Black. With the body of Royal Black. With Royal Black's face. With his strength, but with my brain. Roy Shwartz as the world knew, as Miracle knew, was long dead. So many reach Heaven and start anew. I burst out laughing. Finally, I understood it.

*

But at that moment I was scared. Very scared. I knew some executions had been carried out for breaking into the system. They were illegal, of course, but the system had long ago discarded the rules. It wrote them. People who got in trouble with the system suddenly vanished, fell out of motorboats, had heart attacks, or just got run over. Other people were put in jail for years, went through withdrawal, or underwent disconnecting surgery. And those were people who had only tried to trick the system, to go around the algorithm, to try and compete.

None of them had even dreamed of hacking into Heaven. So no one had gotten the kind of punishment that was waiting for me. I started shivering and sweating. I got up off the chair, panicked, and almost fell back down. I quickly went to the door, to escape, no matter where, no matter how.

Then I stopped. I took a deep breath. "They haven't gotten me yet," I said to myself over and over again. There was still time.

The panic attack passed. I sat on the edge of my bed and started thinking like myself again. Perhaps they had found me out in there, in Heaven, but I wasn't so easy to track here, in reality. I was on a secure Neurox line, secret, closed. I thought - I knew - I had a few more days till they reached me physically. Maybe a little longer. I could still do something. I wasn't just some random teenager. I was trashing Roy Shwartz, the hero who had hacked into Heaven. The only one who had hacked into Heaven!

I could manipulate every existing computer system. I could escape easily. But where to?

Russia was too harsh. Japan was too crowded. China was not an option - they defended themselves too viciously - and Europe was out of the question. True, parts of it were still fine, but the civil war there had not shown any sign of ending, not even after over eighty million casualties. I could escape to Israel, but the proximity to the Caliphate deterred me.

Then I understood where the only safe place for me was.

Maybe dying at seventeen was the solution.

The mist went away.

INSIGHT

I found myself sprawled out on the white floor.

My nose and cheek were almost glued to the smooth texture. My mouth was open and drooling and my head hurt severely. I tried to process the new memories that had just been injected into me. I couldn't. Everything was still mixed, tossed, and vague. The actions that had happened close to when I rose to Heaven were pretty clear, but some of the others, like my childhood, and my mom and dad, were not there. But I knew they would eventually come. Memories are elusive, but you catch them eventually.

I rose on my hands and sat up. My glorious body that I had gotten so used to felt alien to me. I lifted my hand. It was black and muscular, and also pale and chubby. Like double vision. I waved it from side to side. It was unnatural, and yet it was the most natural thing in the world. The sense of duality grew stronger, and it made me dizzy and nauseous.

I remembered when I'd felt like this before. It would happen to me after I played Loom for too many hours straight. I'd have trouble getting back into my body after controlling my avatar, especially when I played a non-human, like a werewolf or a hulk. Often, after two whole days of Loom, I couldn't do anything but unplug my connection to the Neurox and sleep. Sleeping fixed it.

So I closed my eyes. The feeling disappeared. But not like I wanted it to. In my mind, my hand went back to being pink and in need of a tan, my body went back to being heavy and apathetic, and my breathing strenuous, even though I wasn't moving, but only sitting on the floor. I was me, finally. But was it really what I wanted to be?

I opened my eyes and the dizziness came back, but with it a glorious body, strong hands, and steady, even breaths, which I was proud to breathe.

I was me, finally. And, apparently, I was a seventeen-year-old trashing mega-geek. I hadn't thought about my age earlier. Everyone around me in Heaven looked like different versions of age twenty-five, so I felt I was too. On the other hand, I hadn't met anyone there whose real age when they died was less than seventy. Most were closer to one hundred, with a few decades, at least, inside the system. I remembered the Johnsons. Old and wise. Behaving like teenagers in love. Ages are confusing in Heaven.

But... maybe I was really the youngest man in Heaven. Not because I had just arrived up here now.

Now.

Now?

Trash. For a moment, I felt a pulse of fear surge through my body, and I broke out in a cold sweat like I used to when I was the old Roy Shwartz. I jumped to my feet, ignoring the dizziness. I rechecked the data over and over again. Comparing memories and dates.

The numbers were clear: I had uploaded into Heaven on August 18th, 2072. But I had only woken up in Heaven now, January 2nd, 2102.

Thirty years had passed since then. Gone.

Where? What had happened since? Where was my mother?

"I see you found the place," a familiar, melodious voice called out from behind me.

My heart raced. And not with fear.

*

-*"Don't tell me. You two did it."*
-*"I'm being repetitive, huh?"*
-*"Yes."*

*

And still, this time was different. She felt it too.

"Now you can thank me," she said.

"Thank you for what?"

"You were a virgin, before. Right?"

She was right, of course. A week ago, I had been a fat, panting, screechy-voiced geek with untreated acne, and all the social happiness that comes with such baggage. A week ago, I was a complete virgin. In fact, when I thought about it, the first time I had really done it was...

"Trash, right." That's all I had to say. And, "Thank you."

Her smile glowed and her eyes laughed. "You're welcome. And I can assure you. You haven't missed anything down there. It's much better here."

The sweet taste of what we had done mixed with the bitter taste of what I didn't do when I was alive. I couldn't really smile, not for a long time, even though I felt good. The memory of what had happened a week ago, or thirty years ago, mocked me and my feelings.

"Really? I guess I'll never know."

"Trust me. I've done it enough times, with enough people. The best downstairs doesn't compare to the worst here in Heaven."

"If you say so. It's a one-way trip up here."

"Are you sorry about the trip?"

"I didn't have a choice. The police were on the way and I had to come up -" I suddenly stopped. "How did you know I was a virgin?"

"A woman can tell. And... you know, everyone has to come up here. Or they'll die."

I sighed. M had kept her part of the deal. She had told me that when I got here I would find out who I was. Now, obviously, she expected me to tell her. But I wasn't going to do that. Not before I got one important explanation.

"How did you know this place exists? What do you know about me?"

M shrugged. "I didn't know anything about you, other than when you came up to Heaven, something went wrong. For thirty years, you were kept in the system without anyone noticing or taking an interest. You could have been stuck there for a thousand more years."

"How did you find this out?"

"By chance. Your code was stored in the awakening room code, and next to it were instructions to this cave. I was very surprised to find it. I thought I knew everything about Heaven's secrets."

"Apparently not."

"Apparently you're full of surprises."

"Did you try to connect to the handprints there?" I pointed to the wall.

"Of course." A shy expression painted her face. "But nothing happened. It was programmed to respond only to you. And that... that was enough for me to turn you into my personal project."

"And I innocently thought you were just kindhearted."

"I *am* kindhearted!" She was annoyed. "But do you have any idea how many laws I broke for you?"

I remembered the pixies. Maybe there was something to what she said.

M's eyes shimmered with curiosity. "So, tell me! Who are you?"

"The memories are still unclear. But I know, downstairs, my name was Roy."

"Hey, Roy," she said sweetly, and extended her hand for a formal handshake. It felt funny.

"Hey, M." I returned a shy smile. I couldn't give her all my attention even though my body wanted to. Every passing moment unveiled another secret, another memory, another event from the past and my life downstairs. The memories were not easy. All the confidence I had managed to gather here in the past few days started to peel off me. Behind it was a fat high school student who had died a week ago. Trash, why did I need to remember it? Why couldn't I just stay who I was reborn to be?

"And who were you downstairs, Roy? Can you tell me?"

"Not yet," I confessed.

"Is it because of the cops, hmm? Maybe you're a dangerous killer, Roy?"

Me, a killer? I broke out with a thunderous laugh, and then another piece of memory was freed in me and the laugh died. My forehead wrinkled with thoughts, guesses, and efforts to remember. Efforts not to remember. With each passing moment, I hated the moment when I had decided to put my hands against that wall.

M looked at me curiously.

"Wow," she said quietly. "It's a good thing you can't commit murder in Heaven."

"I'm not a murderer," I blurted out quietly.

"But something did happen, down there."

I nodded.

"And it has something to do with those cops you mentioned."

I nodded again, staring at the floor.

"Well, in Heaven there are no cops." Her voice was lighter. She was trying to make me feel better.

"But there are pixies."

"And there are ways around the pixies. I'll teach you how to fight the system."

I looked up at her, and for a moment I thought I was having trouble with my eyesight. She was blurry, unclear. Then my mouth pursed against my will and a smothered sound came out of my throat; I realized I was crying. Tears wet my cheeks and dropped to the floor of the cave. I cried, without resting, without pausing. Because I was in Heaven and I was alone, and even though the most attractive woman in the world sat next to me, all kindhearted and wanting to help, I knew I would always be alone. Thirty years had passed since I had escaped to Heaven. Everyone I knew downstairs, everyone who mattered… they had all been left far behind.

M waited patiently for me to stop. Eventually, I did. I looked at her with appreciation.

"Is that why they don't like you in the system?"

"I don't understand…?"

I tried to explain myself better. "I meant to say, because you teach people how to fight the system - is that why they don't like you?"

She smiled knowingly. "Ah, they have enough reasons not to love me. But that's not about you. They didn't even know about you before you tried to enter the sleep city. Even now, they don't know too much about you."

"There's not much to know about me."

M looked around the cave, at the black handprints, and then back to me.

"You're not much of a liar, Roy."

"Royal. And why would you say such a thing?"

"Because there's a reason that you got stuck in the system for thirty years! Look at those hands on the wall: someone created this place especially for you. Someone thinks you're important."

Someone did, in fact, think so. I sighed.

"It was me. I created it."

M blinked twice.

"When… when did you manage to do that?"

MEMORY 6

The mist came, the mist went away.

I didn't sleep for a week. I took an excessive amount of pills and once every eight hours I put myself in R.E.M. just to keep my sanity, only to go back to the nightmare of the next eight hours. I kept my windows shut. The ventilation system wept. We didn't change the filters all summer. There was no one to take care of it.

Mother knocked on the door. I didn't answer, so she left my meals next to it, on the outside. "You have to stop this," she said from behind the door, and I could hear her crying. "You'll end up killing yourself." What could she possibly know? I didn't tell her anything about my plans. Oh well, she'd find out in a few days anyway. In a few days, she would be left alone in the world. So why ruin the little time she had left?

Eventually, time is the only real thing we have in life. All the rest is what we do with it.

And I didn't have a long time. I had so many things to sort out. Taking care of mother's livelihood for after I was gone was the simplest thing. Five minutes and it was taken care of. She would get a pension for life. I could have done that when I was thirteen, but she wouldn't allow it. She was too proud or too moral or I don't know what, to live like that. Instead, she kept going to her crappy job every day, came home late, ruined her life. Well, no more. Next month she would get a sum that would make her job feel like a bad hobby.

But the most complicated thing was to arrange my own stairway to Heaven. To find a back door. I had visited one of Heaven's absorption centers once. I was curious to know how it looked from the inside. I didn't make it. At the entrance there was an armed military squad. Behind them waited retinal screenings and behind those were five levels of security to go through, up to the cortex level. You had to be rich, filthy rich, to buy yourself an admission ticket to Heaven. Every now and then, all kinds of desperate people, about to die, but unable to fund the procedure, tried to infiltrate it. Sometimes they only tossed them out. Sometimes they sent them to jail. Sometimes it was worse. Only a month before, twelve people had been killed at the entrance to the Houston center.

I suppose if I'd really tried, I would have gotten into one of the centers. But I couldn't stay there long enough. The process - even when you're on the gate of the information and your mind is in the Neurox helmet and your petabytes are jolting - takes more than a full day. And it's a full day of close medical observation, of slow brain death. I could have gotten in, but I would have been exposed after five minutes, tops.

It wasn't the solution for me. I needed to think of another way to cross over. It was the really tricky part. Completely impossible.

*

-"Why?"
-"Because during the boarding process to Heaven, they compress your memories and consciousness into one whole package. It's standard procedure. It takes more than twenty-four hours and at the end of it you are dead. Completely."
-"You couldn't copy the process?"
-"I just didn't have time to program what was needed. Not to mention the broadband I would need. They'd have been onto me."

*

During the formal process, of course, the mind is wiped clean. With me, it had to be different. If I erased myself through the process, who would complete it?

It took me half an hour to crack that problem. It was not an easy or simple solution, but luckily half the project was already ready. It was based on the same principle I'd developed to interface Heaven with my consciousness. If I'd had to reprogram everything from scratch, I wouldn't have made it. I'd have been captured first.

What I did was simple: instead of transferring all my awareness in one go, I found a way to transfer myself in pieces. Memories aside, awareness aside. And true, they're mixed in together. True, no one had ever tried to do that. But I was desperate, I was a trashing genius, and most importantly, it was my only chance.

And for that, I needed a partner, someone to oversee the process. Someone I could trust. There were only two people I could think of: Mother and Jerri.Co. Mother would never have agreed to do it.

That left me one option.

Jerri.Co lived on the other side of America, in one of the warmer regions of Alaska. But of course, no one knew about it. He had been a legend back when I was eight years old, when I had just started messing around with the system more seriously. He was thirty-four then, an activist at heart, officially consulting about network manipulation on the net; unofficially, shamelessly drawing information and money out of them.

I admired him. He had been at the heart of some of the most interesting news of the past few years. When the East Coast's electricity supply started flickering to the beat of Beethoven's Ninth Symphony? It was him. When the Caliphate's water desalination system emptied itself into the ocean? It was him. When all the public holo-systems turned into cartoon versions of themselves? It was him. He had an odd sense of humor, astonishing technical knowledge, and a childish need to bite the system.

When I grew up a little, he started sharing his projects with me. Three years ago, he had added me to the task force he had established, The Robin Goods. We fell apart after a couple of activities, but Jerri.Co and I had stayed friends. I knew he would help me.

So first, I looked for a proper place to stash my memories. I cruised around Heaven for a while, trying to find a place no one would be able to get to. No one would be able to find.

I didn't find such a place. So I just built it. The problem was finding a place that was secret and also one that I, personally, would surely want to go to, even if I didn't know why. So I took the most significant place in Heaven, the place where the rainbow meets the land. There was only one of those and that was enough for me to want it. I dug a cave there, inside the pool. Only a brilliant individual would find out it existed.

I placed my memories there and coded them so only I could get them back.

But I was careful. I only placed my basic memories there. Other information, more sensitive, was stashed elsewhere. Mom always said not to put all my eggs in the same basket. This seemed like a good time to listen to her. But I needed to be very creative in finding hiding spots.

Eventually I connected my Neurox and let the memories flow.

It took a long time.

I always hated waiting. It is frustrating, stupid, and time consuming. And I had to take care of Mom, too, something I had no idea how to do. How could I even talk to her about it? Frustrating, frustrating, frustrating. So, in the meantime, I lay on the bed and tried to imagine how all the knowledge I had, all this genius that made people treat me like a big lump of plutonium, was going up and into the cave.

Naturally, my thoughts wandered to that trash, Miracle Green. Reaching Heaven meant losing her, too. For good. And maybe, I suddenly thought, it didn't have to be forever? I wanted to call her. Make her come to me and then convince her to go with me to Heaven. Who knows? Maybe she would have gone for it. All in all, life was pretty shitty for her too.

Of course, I didn't do it. Maybe I was seventeen, maybe I had a crush on someone who would never notice me, but I wasn't completely crazy. It was enough to imagine the cops knocking down my door to prevent me from even talking to her about it. But then a new hope arrived. Maybe I would meet her there in Heaven? If that were to happen, it would happen many years from now. I was seventeen, and she wasn't planning on dying in the next hundred years. Still, if and when that happened... I had a feeling it would be very interesting.

I promised myself I would wait for her.

The mist went away.

EXIT

"You can close your mouth now," I told M.

She closed it, but didn't look less surprised. I couldn't stop looking at her. Her perfect legs were pulled to her chest, her chin was resting on her knees. Her eyes glittered with curiosity.

"You still insist you aren't special?"

"Right now I'm just an idiot looking for his memory. Maybe when I find it, I'll feel differently."

"But you already found it, didn't you?"

"Just a small part of it. The other parts, apparently, are scattered all over Heaven."

"What? Why?"

I got up off the floor and stretched my limbs. I felt much better, but also much worse. On the one hand, for the first time since I woke up in Heaven, I knew who I was and what I needed to do. I had a memory of myself. But on the other hand, the more I remembered, the more I knew how important the things I couldn't remember were - the black holes in my memory, the ones I had personally hidden in Heaven, for reasons I didn't know. I felt the way you feel after a particularly long visit to the dentist. You know your mouth is there, but you can't feel it.

For the first time in thirty years, I felt hungry. And not hungry for food.

"Come on. We're going."

I didn't wait for her. I turned around and walked quickly down the tunnel. Behind me came a surprised shout and, after it, fast, barefoot footsteps. A curve, two, and I reached the blue hole leading to the color pool, to the massive downward currents. I didn't even bother jumping into the opening. I just beamed forward and then up, up, and up again. The fourth time took me out of the pool, right next to the rainbow.

*

-"I always loved rainbows."
-"You should see the one in Heaven. See, there are a lot of amazing places

98

there. But there, at the end of the rainbow, at the biggest and most colorful waterfall ever made, with swirling, delicious, color clouds a hundred feet tall, where the emerald jungle invades the color pool – that's the most beautiful place you will ever see."

*

"You can close your mouth now," she finally said.

I stood there for over a minute in complete silence. I couldn't do anything but look at this color display in awe. I tried to remember if I'd been there before, before I came up to Heaven. Did I visit there as an unseen ghost? Maybe I had, but the memory of it just wasn't there. A lot of memories were missing.

"I don't remember where I put them."

"Put what? Your memories?"

I nodded. It had to be somewhere close. From what I'd discovered about myself, I knew I'd have left myself clues. It just had to be close, in plain sight, but couldn't be obvious. Something only I would understand. Something only I would notice. I looked all around. Maybe inside the pool? At the bottom? No, that was too obvious. Not creative enough, either. If the cave that had my first memory was in the pool, there was no chance I would have kept the rest of the treasure next to it.

Perhaps in one of the colors? I approached the edge of the pool, examining the giant waterfall falling into it. I didn't notice that something had started changing in the scenery. I was that focused.

"Let's get out of here," M suddenly said. Her voice was a little odd. Tense.

I still didn't respond. I tried to concentrate on the rainbow. I was sure it had something to do with it, somehow. Maybe something in the colors? Between the colors? The shape? The colorful foam over the pool?

"What are we waiting for?" she shouted over the colors' hiss, pulling at my hand. I pulled it back.

"I'm looking for colors that aren't supposed to be in the rainbow!" I yelled back.

"But the rainbow has all the colors!" she yelled again. "There's nothing here!"

I felt no desire to answer her. Without my memories, without that thing I was missing, I felt very vulnerable. Somewhere out there, I knew, there was a swarm of pixies searching for me. And perhaps not just the pixies. The system had tagged me as an unwanted factor; it was only a matter of time before it caught me again.

I had to hurry.

I had to hurry.

MEMORY 7

The mist came, the mist went away.

A knock on the door woke me up.

I was just finishing an R.E.M. session, breaking free from another disturbing dream about my father. He was dressed in an orange outfit, and someone dressed in black, with a mask, stood beside him with a curved blade. I knew what was going to happen and I wanted to jump on him and prevent it, but I was five years old and all I could do was throw grass at him.

I hated that nightmare. Usually I could avoid it, but I was lacking too many hours of real sleep to fight it. When dream sleep is unnatural, the brain projects its distress in other ways. That was the price and I, unhappily, paid it.

The hard knock on the door ended that nightmare and brought me back to a reality just as scary. Mom wouldn't knock on my door for no reason. She always had a good enough reason and this time the reason could be only one thing: a bunch of armed police officers, coming to take her son away, never to be heard from again. I had to get up, I had to run away. But I knew I had nowhere to run to; I had no ability to do it even if I could.

I rolled out of bed and fell on the floor. The pain woke me up a little. I crawled on all fours to the door and then climbed up it and opened it.

"Roy, there's a woman here to see you," Mother told me. "She says it's very important."

Next to her was an adult woman. At first glance, she didn't look much over forty. At second glance too. Only later did I notice all the plastic surgery she had gone through. It was amazing. Almost every part of her body was fake. In those cases, they called it a full-body implant: gradual replacement of all the organs, replacing a different one each time. With the cheap versions, they got a bionic prosthetic; the expensive types got an organic prosthetic, or in her case, cloned organs, born out of the original tissue. In the end, you keep only your brain.

She was rather short. A beautiful woman with yellow hair, a white smile, and piercing blue eyes.

"Roy Schwartz, right?" She extended her hand.

Without understanding what I was doing, I shook her hand. She turned around, looked at my mother's amazed face, and closed the door on her. I was groggy enough to play along. But in my heart, I started to hate her.

"What... why?" I mumbled.

"Are you the one who wants to go up to Heaven?"

In an instant I was wide awake.

"I will help you," she said in a pleasant voice, and pushed me back to the bed. I didn't have the strength to resist. From within the pillows, I watched as she examined the room, checking out the computer system that was in the corner, the pile of components stacked on the table next to it, the Neurox helmet, the Leprechaun poster I had over my bed. With skilled fingers, she felt the physical joint of my connection to the net, through the wall, and nodded appreciatively. Rightly so, of course.

Eventually she came back to me and looked at me from above.

"Did you really think you'd go undetected, Kiddo?"

I didn't answer. I still didn't understand what this woman was doing in my room and where exactly she was hiding the squad of police officers that was supposed to take me to be erased.

"You thought you could hack into Heaven and do whatever you wanted in there?" she repeated. I still didn't know what to answer.

Eventually, she took a pile of clothes from my bed and tossed it on the floor, sitting in its place.

"Relax. They don't know who you are." She smiled cunningly. "I changed the tracker's information. They think you're in New Delhi."

I was so tired that I didn't take the meaning of her words to heart. Slowly I started to understand that the police would not be arriving today after all.

"I want to go back to sleep," I mumbled and closed my eyes.

*

-"Great timing."

-"This time I didn't go into R. E. M. - I didn't have a chance to. I just slipped into calm, blessed sleep. A sleep I lacked. If there's one thing I miss from downstairs, it's the ability to sleep. Here, you're never really sleeping. You unload, you get clean, you freshen up... but you don't sleep. I'd give everything for a good night's sleep."

102

*

I woke up approximately twenty hours later, with the taste of glue in my mouth. I wanted to get up, brush my teeth, and wash up, but the scratching noises from the corner of my room made me stop and stare. Her implant body was there, connected to my Neurox, logged into my system, and scraping my chair with a sharp knife. Her face had a smile that reminded me of a skull.

"Who are you?" I asked.

She took off the helmet and slowly logged out of the system. Her eyes became clear and her pupils focused, her smile became more human.

"You can call me Melissa," she said, aiming the hand with the knife at me. A second later, she giggled, switched the knife to the other hand, and reached her right hand out to shake. She liked shaking hands, it seemed.

But this time, I did not shake her hand. At this point, I realized that I was in no immediate danger, and this woman was probably responsible for that. I appreciated it, but I didn't like the fact that she had gotten into my room. Suddenly, I asked myself how she had even done that.

"My mother...?"

"She's fine, Roy. I can call you Roy, right? I gave her some money to get us some food. It stinks in here, you know."

"I'm going to take a shower."

For a moment, I didn't know how I was going to strip next to her, but then I looked at her again and took off all my clothes without a second thought. I needed the time in the shower to think, anyway. Melissa, Melissa...

"Are you *the* Melissa?" I asked when I got out of the shower, dripping on the floor.

"In the flesh." She smiled widely, an artificial, ugly smile that made me look the other way.

Trash. I didn't know Melissa was even still alive. There were rumors about her retiring to some tropical island and other rumors about her working on another project with The Face Company. But I was certain those were rumors. Because Melissa should be about - I did a quick calculation - 130 years old. I looked at her with new wonder.

"So what do you want from me?"

"Isn't it obvious?" She spread her implanted hands out to the sides. "A place in Heaven!"

MONSTER

The scenery around me changed, but I didn't notice it. I was hypnotized by the rainbow. For a few minutes I tried to find some clue in it to lead me forward, and I didn't feel how it was changing me. The deeper I looked into it, the more colors I found. A lot more colors than regular rainbows. The constant flow of colors downward, the colors mixing in the pool, their amazing richness... gave me peace. And, I realized, that was what I was missing.

That, and my memory, of course.

Because Heaven is supposed to be a peaceful place. After the vulnerable, insecure life down there, when you go to Heaven, you should feel serene. Because you did it. You survived death! You have nothing to fear anymore. You don't get injured anymore, you don't have to hurt anymore, and you are not obligated to be anywhere. Trash, you did it! Your second life is before you and it's not going to end.

A whole world, a whole universe of new experiences and new pleasures, waiting for you.

*

-*"You sound like a commercial for Heaven. The system's commercial."*
-*"But that's how it should be here."*
-*"And isn't it?"*

*

M punched my shoulder. Again and again.

And again.

"What?" I finally snapped. I tore my gaze away from the rainbow. My shoulder hurt. I wondered how long M had been punching me.

"Did you hear that?"

"Hear what?"

"Back there, in the trees."

Her hand was shaking. She pointed to a spot in the jungle. I glanced at the rainbow one last time and tried to understand why it was so important for her to disturb me. At first I didn't hear anything, of course. The noise from the waterfall was too loud. But then I found out I could just ignore it. Shut it off. I did that, and what was left of the serene illusion was completely gone.

At once, I found that the jungle's vibe had changed. Suddenly I was surrounded by odd noises, unfamiliar and unpleasant. Sharp leaves moved with the wind, bustling like knives. Branches knocked together. All kinds of insects hummed. From somewhere in the distance came the sounds of a chase, roars, and after that a terrible scream of pain and hungry gnawing sounds. Birds chirped in deformed voices. The more I focused, the scarier it got. Something in this jungle was off. And something, I suddenly knew, was looking at me.

"Do you feel it too?" M asked. It was the first time I heard her voice tense.

"Yes. Is it supposed to be like this?"

"I was only here once before, when I found the cave. I felt the same thing. I don't think people are meant to come here."

"Why?"

My sense of fear rapidly grew. Something was here, in this jungle, I just knew it. That something was hungry and cruel. Part of me wanted to run away, disappear, but the rational side held me there by force. You cannot die in Heaven, I silently chanted over and over again. You can't die. I still searched for what was growling and clattering behind the first row of trees, but I wasn't sure I wanted to find it anymore.

"I don't know. The thing is, no one ever comes here."

"Are there other places like this in Heaven?"

"Not like this. I want to get out of here."

I looked at her. She seemed a little scared, agitated. And, as impossible as it might seem, paler than ever. It made me laugh a little, despite the growing sense of terror.

"You can go as far as I'm concerned."

She threw me an angry look. "Don't forget who brought you here."

"Don't worry. From now on I intend to remember everything."

The rattling sounds grew louder and were suddenly very close. Something huge moved among the trees, shaking them, but still hidden from sight. The air around us turned stale, filled with scents of decay and death. My body tensed, muscles wanting to run away, escape, get as far away from there as possible. But I held on. M slipped her hand into mine and we clung together.

A deep, growling voice shook the world around us, as if we were next to the jaws of a hungry, predatory dinosaur. The trees around us started to collapse, trunks cracked open as if they were toothpicks.

That was all we needed. We jumped back, terrified, and started running toward the other side of the jungle.

*

-*"Why didn't you beam out?"*
-*"You can only beam to where you can see. In the jungle, you can't see more than a few feet ahead."*

*

Entering the tree line put us through a world of smacking branches, tripping roots, and razor-sharp leaves doing everything to get into my eyes. My body was soon covered with burning cuts, but I couldn't stop running. The roars behind me didn't stop and were now accompanied by heavy hooves galloping just a few feet behind me. I kept hearing the trees cracking and falling. I developed a crazy running speed. Never in my life had I been more scared than I was in those moments.

M was thundering next to me on a parallel course, keeping the same speed. I managed to look at her every now and then. Her beautiful pale body was covered with long, red scratches. Her hair was flowing behind her and got caught in the branches every now and then. She was focused on avoiding obstacles and evading the roots that were trying so hard to catch her. Her face was crooked and tense. I wondered if I looked the same.

Then the tree line opened and we broke out into... a colorful, magical pool of colors, into which a mighty rainbow waterfall spilled. We were running in circles. We looked at each other in despair. There was nowhere to run anymore.

Behind us there was a roar, closer than ever now. We turned around, bracing ourselves.

*

Out from the tree line came an angry, panting leprechaun. He was a little over three feet tall. He wore a green suit and a top hat tied with a bow. His eyebrows were furrowed. He walked toward me and stopped. His eyes were shooting daggers.

"You piece of trash!" he screamed. "Thirty years I have waited for you in this dump. Thirty years!"

He stretched up on his toes, jumped in the air, and slapped me.

MEMORY 8

The mist came, the mist went away.

I burst out laughing.

I needed it. After all the tension, after all that had happened in the past few weeks, the preparations, the lack of sleep, and the despair I slipped into whenever I thought the police had finally caught me, I totally needed it. The old lady just wanted to go to Heaven. That's all!

That is trashing all. But there was one thing I couldn't figure out.

"Why do you need me to get into Heaven?"

She looked at me in disbelief, started to say something, paused, started again, and then extended her hands to the sides trying to explain the obvious. Suddenly she looked her real age – 130, almost completely refurbished, packed with medications, implants, and a desperate attempt to hold on to every second of life her money could buy. And money, I knew, was something she had more of than almost anyone else in the world.

"Because Rage won't let me."

She looked down at her shoes, ashamed. Indeed, there was reason to be ashamed. I knew the story of Rage and Melissa. The prince against the queen mother, the son versus the lover, the heir against the business rival. Anyone who had ever had some link to technology knew the story. Movies were made about it. It was a romantic comedy of mistakes, or emotional tragedy, or business rivalry getting out of all proportion and control. Couldn't tell the difference anymore.

I never understood how people who have everything, truly everything, can fight over honor like that. Over influential territories. The legal battle over Heaven was all or nothing. In the end, one would have everything, and the other was going to lose everything. Truly everything.

"Is this his way of getting back at you?" I asked.

"Another spoiled brat, playing with the toys his daddy built him."

I agreed with what she said. Since Heaven had been established, things had changed. Controlling information was one thing. Indexing the world was another. But to promise eternal life was a whole different thing. A different kind of power.

"But don't worry, Kiddo. We're going to change that, you and I."

"How?"

"I've already told you, haven't I? You're going to get me into Heaven, and fast."

*

-"*You? Get her in? You?*"

-"*That's what she wanted. And suddenly I understood that it was all that had been occupying her the past few years. Trying to hack into Heaven, to get in there by some back door. Do what I was going to do.*"

-"*But you're talking about trashing Melissa. She had unlimited resources! She could hire the best programming team money can buy! Why did she come to you, of all people?*"

-"*Because I was the only one in the world that could do it.*"

*

"I can't do that."

Her eyes lit up threateningly. "I know you can. I've been following you for months."

I was still dripping on the floor. I didn't want to get into an argument at that moment, but I couldn't deny her an answer. "It doesn't change the facts. To get into Heaven, you have to go through one of Heaven's gates. True, I hacked the system, but I'm only visiting there, that's all."

Melissa probably knew better. She wouldn't have come to me if she wasn't sure of her visit. But she wasn't going to argue with me either. She was one hundred and thirty and I was seventeen, but time was still on her side.

"If so," she said, "I have no reason to hold off the cops anymore. They'll be here in ten minutes."

Threats don't work well on me. I mean, bad threats don't work well on me. After I didn't respond to her, she repeated her words in an even more threatening tone. She even stressed her intent by waving her finger in front of me.

"Is that what you want, Schwartz? They'll be here in ten minutes!"

She closed her eyes, her pupils moved. I knew she was opening a line of communication, but I didn't know to whom. The police?

"You won't go to the police, Melissa. You're already doing

110

something illegal."

"I don't need to go to the police. Do you know how badly Rage wants to know how you've been sneaking into Heaven, and what he's willing to give me for it?"

Everything, I thought to myself. He would give her everything. She had won. At that moment I forgot I was nude, I forgot I was wet and so was the floor. Still, she was a 130-year-old lady; what she had in years, I had in pounds. I thought I could take her out in a second. I would have to take her out. I no longer cared about the police. But if I killed her fast enough, they wouldn't get to me in time. I lunged at her.

With a flaccid, fat body that panted while sitting, it was hard for me to move fast.

She was a lot more agile than I was. In fact, even if I'd been in shape, she'd probably have been quicker than I was. Because all she did was open her palm, and the last thing I saw clearly was a flash of electricity coming from her.

*

-*"Implants! You never know what they have in there."*

-*"In retrospect, I should have expected her to do something like that. I knew almost every part of her body had been replaced at least once. So why wouldn't she get modifications here and there, for self-defense?"*

-*"A woman of her stature needs to know self-defense."*

-*"Exactly. That's what I'd have done myself, if I'd remained living downstairs. If I'd had enough money."*

*

I found myself on the floor, convulsing and shaking uncontrollably. My eyes saw darkness, my head bounced against the hard floor, but I didn't lose consciousness. I just lay there, helpless.

"You white trashing fat ass," I heard her cussing quietly. "You try to raise your hand to me? Rude. The police will make jarred pickles out of you. I will personally see it happen."

I had to stop her.

"Wait... wait a minute..." I gurgled.

"Stay on the floor and shut up. I knew it was a mistake to come

111

here. You're just an advanced script kid, that's all. No talent at all."

"Trash you!" I cursed.

"Trash yourself, mothertrasher." She had colorful language, the old hag. More so, she had experience. Today I knew she had just learned what triggered me and pushed the right button. She had gone through a lifetime of managing super-programmers who thought quasars shone out of their asses.

"I can get you into Heaven," I blurted angrily, writhing on the floor.

"I don't believe you. You're too… ordinary."

*

-*"Too ordinary?"*
-*"That, apparently, was all she needed to say to me."*

*

It took me less than a week to adapt my system to her brain. I used some new tricks she taught me and linked her to the improvised gate I built to Heaven. I could transfer her consciousness and memory together, in the regular process. I was there to finish it. Another thing happened during that week: we started talking. And when you talk, you find out things about one another. She told me some juicy stories about some computerization legends that had worked by or under her, and I shared my problems with Miracle Green and Mother. She told me what had really happened with Rage; I showed her old photos of me and Father.

By the time the process started, I was rather fond of her. She lay on my bed with her head in my helmet and her eyes staring into mine.

"You're a good kid, Schwartz," she said, as the process went into the final stages.

I smiled. I could almost hear her consciousness flowing out of her body. Soon, I knew, she wouldn't be able to speak. I placed my hand over hers and she squeezed it hungrily.

"How do you feel?"

"Weed." And after a few seconds, "Lots of weed."

I looked at her. A hundred years ago, she had been a very beautiful woman. Pretty and regal. I had to admit, up to her last moment, she retained her nobility. In the week I'd known her, we'd never stopped talking. I discovered an enchanting and clever woman, who knew exactly what she wanted and did everything to get it. I loved that about her. I also loved her generosity. She was always giving compliments. She bore no jealousy. She was everything Miracle Green was supposed to be, but with extra experience. Perhaps it was because of that extra experience.

"I'd take you, Kiddo," she mumbled, and her eyes lost focus.

She stopped breathing a few hours later.

The mist has gone away.

LEPRECHAUN

The slap hurt, but at the same time, for some reason, the jungle stopped being scary. The frightening sounds stopped, the roaring was gone, even the smells were nicer. There was only the pool behind us and the spectacular waterfall of color above us. M and I stood there, shocked, and the leprechaun cursed and swore and screamed. His face turned red with anger.

"You said it would take a few hours! Hours! And you dare come here after thirty years! Have you no shame?"

He jumped up for another jump-slap. But this time I was prepared. This time I caught him by the throat and held him before me in midair, out of the range of his fists. He tried to kick me, but my arm was longer than his legs, too.

"Either you calm down, or I'm going to drown you in the pool," I said.

He ceased for a moment and then bit my hand. He had sharp teeth, but I kept holding on. Eventually I dunked him in the color pool. I didn't really know how he would respond, but air bubbles started rising from below and he struggled harder.

I pulled him out of the pool. He coughed and spit the color out of his mouth.

"Are you going to calm down?"

The leprechaun gave me an angry look, but stopped his tantrum.

"Yes, Master. I am sorry about this, Master."

Master? I let him down easy, expecting him to start attacking me again. But he just squeezed the color out of his white beard, pulled a pipe out of his coat pocket, stuffed it with tobacco, and started blowing smoke rings. When he pulled the pipe out of his mouth he seemed a lot calmer.

"Why did you wait so long, Master?"

I didn't get a chance to answer before M jumped in. "Why are you calling him master?"

The Leprechaun looked at her for a moment, eyeing her, then looked back to me. "Why did you wait so long, Master?"

I sat by him, so I could look into his eyes on his level. Why did he call me Master? It was obvious he knew who I was. And if he had really waited for me here for thirty years, how was that possible?

I, on the other hand, had no idea at all who he was.

"What's your name?"

"How should I know? You never bothered naming me."

"Charlie, then. Your name is Charlie."

The leprechaun smiled, looking relieved. "Charlie is good. So what took you so long?"

"So, here's the thing, Charlie. I don't know why it took me so long. Perhaps you could help me with it?"

"Of course, Master. That is why I exist! To help you."

I looked at him. He looked at me. M looked at him, then at me. I looked at M and then turned my gaze back to Charlie. He blew a white smoke ring up and looked content.

"Well?"

"Well, what?" Charlie raised an eyebrow.

"What do you know about me being held up?"

Charlie blew another smoke ring. "I do not know. If I had known, I would not have asked you. Right, Master?"

"You don't have to call me Master, Charlie. Call me by my real name."

"Master is not your real name?"

M giggled at my side. I looked at her to see if maybe she was making any sense of what I could not, but she just shrugged. I turned back to Charlie.

"You can call me Black. Royal Black."

"Royal Black! How clever of you, Master Black."

"And now you can help me."

"Help you with what, Master Black?"

My patience was running thin. "Help me with what you were supposed to help me with!"

"Ah! You mean the treasure?"

Inside, I was jumping with joy, but outside, not even a single muscle moved.

"Yes, Charlie, the treasure."

"So why did you not just ask?"

I thought I was losing my mind. "Charlie, I'm asking you to -"

The leprechaun didn't wait to hear it. He turned on his heels quickly and, within a fraction of a second, had charged into the jungle. I rushed behind him, M rushed behind me. I couldn't help but think about how different the walk through the jungle was this time.

Only a few minutes ago, I had run through it, terrified; now I could enjoy the chirping birds and the stroking leaves.

"Are you responsible for the change in the jungle?"

He turned his face to me without slowing down and without walking into any trees. On his face was a sly smile. "I am only following orders, Master Black," he said, speeding up his pace.

MEMORY 9

The mist came, the mist went away.

Getting rid of Melissa's body was not going to be simple at all.

That's why I didn't do it. I just wrapped her up in a big black trash bag, the kind you use for raking leaves. Then another one, and another one. I cleared out everything I had in the refrigerator in my room, put her inside, and closed it. I knew at some point she would be discovered, but when that happened, I planned to have been dead for a while.

As for Mom, she was a bigger problem. Melissa was one thing. I could sell Mom something about the old lady vanishing. But at some point I needed to tell her about me and my plans. I couldn't let her deal with the moment I went from being her beloved child to being a rotting slab of meat, alone.

I considered my options.

On the one hand, I could buy her a plane ticket to somewhere. Set her up with a comfortable, anonymous life in another country. But that, of course, wasn't the real problem. What would she do, all alone in the world? How would she live? What would she remember about me? And how sad and broken hearted would she be, with her son dead? That was the problem. Not to mention the fact that the minute the government found out what I had done, they would want to question my mother. And if, after that, there was anything left of her, the system would destroy her. Above the need to suck every piece of information from her, it was just their principle. Deterrence.

There was a second option. But for that I had to do something I hadn't done in years: actually talk to Mom.

*

-"*That must have been hard.*"

-"*A lot easier than I thought. I think she was just happy to talk to me again after all these years. But there were tears, and not just hers. I explained the situation to her. She looked at me with misty eyes and just nodded. I told her about hacking into Heaven, how I'd been discovered. I told her who the old lady was who had visited me (she already knew) and why she was now in the fridge in*

117

a plastic bag. I told her about my plans to escape."
-"Then what?"
-"Then I asked her what she wanted to do."

*

"Take me with you," she said, without hesitation.

And that was it. For a moment I had thought I'd have to fight to convince her. But in my opinion, she had just been waiting for something like this to happen. Since my father had died on the battlefield, she hadn't really had a life. A 45-year-old woman, a beautiful 45-year-old woman whose one, great love who had been butchered in the battle for France, with an antisocial genius child who escaped into his own world, a dead-end job, and friends who deserted her when things became hard. If there was a woman who needed to leave this world urgently, it was Mom.

It took me a couple more days to rig the system for her. I worked as fast as I could. I had to hurry because now, because with Melissa no longer in the picture, there was no one to stop the authorities from locating me. And they were on their way, I was sure of that. And still I had to work with the utmost precision. Otherwise, the process would fail. And I didn't have time. There was no time!

"Mom," I told her when she was wearing the helmet, "I need to tell you something."

She looked at me.

"I can't transfer you into Heaven in the ordinary way."

She closed her eyes for a long second and then reached her hand out to unplug herself from the equipment.

"No, no!" I cried and grabbed her hand. She looked at me, puzzled.

"What I mean is that I have to compress you and send you there in a packet. You won't wake up in Heaven immediately. I'll have to come and extract you from the packet."

She closed her eyes again. "Will I feel anything?" she asked.

"No, it will feel just the same as it normally would. You'll fall asleep here and wake up there."

She smiled.

*

-"Yeah, sometimes I'm a little bit of an idiot."

*

From that moment on it was easier.

Mom called everyone who needed to be called. She pre-made sandwiches for me for the days to come ("Who'll take care of you when I'm gone? You?") and eventually put herself in the plastic bags, to save me from having to do it. I blessed her for it. If there was one thing I really wanted to avoid, it was putting my mother in a trash bag.

I connected her to the system and watched her as her consciousness faded. Near the end she looked at me, smiled, and closed her eyes. Her breathing became shallow. The system was working at a steady pace and my mother was fading away from me.

Even though I knew I'd see her on the other side, I couldn't help but break down. Something about the end of all this, I think, was what did it. Mother was halfway to Heaven, and she was never coming back to this world. The world I was stuck in. The world I had to get out of.

It took me almost three hours to get past the tears.

Eventually I got in the shower, and when I got out, I was calmer. The house was very quiet and I went to get the Easter eggs I had created for myself. It was an idea that only blossomed after I had thought about mother's packet, but it was fairly obvious. If I could send her to Heaven, I could send other things to Heaven as well.

In fact, there was no way I would go to Heaven without preparing a few tricks in advance. The more I thought about it, the more I liked the idea.

Those 'few tricks' were quite a lot of strings of code, some very complex. Eventually I got the core code of Heaven packed into one of the eggs. I didn't know what I could even do with it, but I wanted it to be under my control.

So I used the spare time I had and went on another journey into Heaven. A final journey as an observer with a bag full of treasures for the honest seeker. And, more importantly, ways to hide them from the dishonest seeker.

The mist came, the mist went away.

EASTER EGG

"Are you taking me to Mother?" I shouted.

The journey through the jungle had been going on for a few minutes now at a crazy speed, and I wanted to know where the leprechaun was leading us. I wanted to know a lot of things, really. First and foremost, I wanted to know where Mother's packet was. For some reason, her location was not in my memory, at least not in those that had returned to me. Maybe the leprechaun knew where she was? Even though I didn't remember him, either, it was obvious he was linked to me in some way. I must have created him. And if I had created him, perhaps I had made him guard Mother's packet.

"No!" he shouted back at me without even looking, and picked up the pace. His little feet became a blur and his heels spattered stems and roots straight into my eyes. I suspected he was aiming them there on purpose.

"So where are we going?"

"You will see, you will see," he chuckled, and bounced to the right. We kept moving among the trees at high speed. He was leading, I was behind him, and M was behind me. The jungle had no visible road, but Charlie knew exactly where he was going. Of course, he always chose to go under the shortest branches, laughing as he did, and once he even jumped into a hollow tree trunk, making M and me crawl on our elbows, sinking in white worm slime, just to get through to the other side and keep going through the jungle.

"I swear," M was panting behind me, "I'm going to rip his -"

"Get in line," I answered.

Finally, we arrived. Charlie stopped suddenly and I had to make a conscious effort not to smash into him. M, at the other end, crashed into me from behind. It was pleasant.

I cleaned the dirt and spiders' webs off my face. I looked around. A jungle. Just like the jungle we'd been in ten minutes ago. Tall trees, low bushes, wide leaves, dirt, an excessive amount of insects… just nothing.

"There." Charlie pointed at one of the trees proudly. "There is one of the treasures."

It was a large tree that at first glance looked the same as every other tree around me. I walked up to it and examined it closely. It smelled like any other tree. It had bark like any other tree. When I broke a piece of it off, sap leaked out, crusting in the air.

"That's the treasure? Are you sure?" I asked the leprechaun.

"Of course I am sure," he answered, sitting down next to where I stood, then re-lighting the tobacco in his pipe. "Here is the treasure. The treasure is here."

"Inside the tree? Next to the tree? Under the tree?"

"I do not know, Master. All I know is that it is here."

In the meantime, M had climbed up the tree. Her pale face peeked out from within the green branches. "There's nothing here. He must be toying with you. Maybe he was lying to you from the start? Maybe he doesn't know you at all..."

Charlie listened to her but chose not to respond. I chose otherwise.

"Is that true, Charlie?"

"What?"

"That you don't really know me. That you're just playing with us."

The leprechaun choked in the middle of blowing a smoke ring. He coughed, threw the pipe on the ground, and jumped to his feet.

"Thirty years! Thirty years I wait here for you, scaring people away, counting the seconds! And you - when you finally arrive, you have the nerve to pretend that you do not know who I am! And bring all kinds of... those!" He waved in the general direction of M. "So who is playing who, you tell me! Who is playing whom?"

His face turned crimson and for a moment the jungle around us went back to being scary.

"Relax. Calm down." I placed my hand on his shoulder. "I'm just suffering from temporary memory loss. That's why I didn't get here on time. I appreciate the fact you waited for me, Charlie. I appreciate it a lot."

"Really?" he squeaked submissively. The crimson shade started leaving his face.

"Truly." I leaned down and looked at him at his eye level. "I need your help, Charlie. I need it more than ever. I believe the treasure is here, around here. I just don't know how to reach it. You have to tell me."

"Alright," he agreed, then lifted his pipe and lit it once more. He pointed to M again. "But she should not be here."

"What do you mean I shouldn't be here?" M jumped down from

121

the tree and screamed at him. "How rude! You don't even know who I am! You drag us into this -"

He blew a smoke ring in her face.

*

-"Haha! I just love him."
-"Yes, the little shit had courage. And attitude. I was loving him more and more with each passing moment."

*

M just froze in anger. It took her, perhaps, a fraction of a second to snap out of it, and then her right hand swung up quickly and connected with a loud slap on the leprechaun's left cheek. Charlie flew a few feet back, rolled over, came back up, fell again, and eventually was stopped by a bush.

"She should not be here, Master," he repeated in an accusatory voice from afar. Then he broke down, crying. Tears just sprang out of his eyes like a fountain, like in one of those cartoons from the last century. His eyes turned red.

I looked at M, puzzled. Why did she have to slap him? Suddenly she looked completely different. Like a stranger. The leprechaun kept crying; it was obvious he wasn't going to show me what I wanted as long as she was around.

"Maybe you should give us a few minutes together."

M was seething; I could see tiny streaks of lightning under her skin. For a moment it looked like I was going to get slapped too. But she took a deep breath, calmed down, and nodded her head.

"Five minutes. Five minutes and I'm back."

She took her dignity and with a regal step disappeared between the jungle trees.

"Further!" Charlie called behind her. He was no longer crying.

Eventually he came close to me and quirked a thick brow.

"You have to walk around the tree four times, then crow like a rooster."

Silence.

"Why are you looking at me like that, Master Black? Those were your instructions, not mine!"

122

MEMORY 10

The mist came, the mist went away.

The house was empty. My footsteps echoed.

Mom was deep in the fridge, next to Melissa's body. Although I'd never had a problem being alone - preferred it, in fact - this was different. Loneliness is a great choice, but a lousy constraint. I turned the old holovision on to chase it away. In the background, they reported riots in London and another virus in Africa, but I don't remember much beyond that. I was busy.

Something had happened to my hardware after I had uploaded Mom to Heaven. I needed to recalibrate it, adjust it to myself. It took a while, a while I knew I didn't have. For lack of any other option, I went back to R.E.M. sessions to prolong my waking hours. After the second treatment, the nightmares came back; this time they were not only about Dad, but Mom too. In the dream, she was buried in a sand dune, closed up in a glass coffin. She screamed something to me that I couldn't understand, trying to break the glass with her fists. But she couldn't crack it and I tried to find a rock big enough to free her. The problem was that there was nothing but sand all around. Eventually I found a rock, but I was afraid to use it. I knew the breaking glass would injure Mom. Nightmare.

When I woke up from those nightmares, they were not completely gone. For hours I could hear Mom's imaginary screams from inside her glass coffin.

All the fresh food in the house ran out. I wasn't in the mood to eat anyway. I opened a few old cans. Pickles, mushrooms, pumpkin soup. After I finished eating them, I didn't bother throwing them in the trash can. I wasn't going to stay in this house for long anyway. After a few days I even stopped putting them in the corner. I just tossed them to the other side of the room and when the corner was overflowing, I tossed them into the hallway.

Soon the house started to look like Earth: dirty, contaminated, as if a teenager that wasn't going to live more than a few days was living there. But I didn't care. I immersed myself in my technology and the hell with the world. A few minor adjustments and this would all be behind me.

When everything was ready, I contacted Jerri.Co. I had informed him earlier that I was working on something big and that I would need his help. I didn't share all the details with him. He didn't ask for them. I knew his mind was working and he alone would understand. The line was secure, but that didn't mean anything. The system didn't think it was possible to hack into Heaven, either. I asked Jerri.Co to supervise the process remotely. To turn off the lights when I went to sleep. To disconnect me.

I needed someone to do it for me.

The last thing I remembered from downstairs was the last time I went to the bathroom. I didn't flush the toilet. It made me laugh. Later I lay in bed, in the spot where Melissa and later on, Mother, had lain. I connected myself to the Neurox.

I wondered what state of decomposition the police would find me in. Would they realize what I had done, or just think I had murdered Melissa and Mom and then committed suicide?

And then, slowly, everything went dark. I started flowing out of my body, through Heaven's gates.

The mist came.

TREE

It felt odd.

Not because I really did circle the tree four times and then crowed like a rooster. I'd done stupider things in my life. I mean, I imagined I had. I didn't really remember. It felt odd because of Charlie.

The merry leprechaun sat on a rock, smoked his endless pipe, and stared at me shrewdly. He didn't take his eyes off me.

I walked around the tree once, and I felt his smile grow a little. Other than that, nothing happened. I huffed in frustration and promised myself that if I was making a fool out of myself for no reason, he was going to suffer.

After the second time around the tree, nothing happened either. Other than his smile growing that much wider, and instead of smoke rings he started blowing out smoke triangles. On my part, I realized how useless it was to try to make him suffer. He was a leprechaun, after all. And a virtual leprechaun, at that. An AI. He couldn't really suffer. Aside from that, I decided I rather liked him.

After the third time around I stopped liking him. The smoke triangles turned into squares and his smile turned into a chuckle. I realized I was walking around a meaningless tree in the middle of the jungle simply because a devious leprechaun was taking advantage of my innocence. It was one of the most embarrassing moments to ever go down in human history. I wanted to stop the farce, but I kept going. I knew if I stopped Charlie would yell at me that I'd have to, "Start over, Master." And I, like a good Master, would, of course, start all over again.

I made the fourth circle quickly. The leprechaun wasn't blowing any smoke rings. He couldn't. The pipe had fallen out of his hand earlier, and he was holding his stomach, laughing. I cursed quietly and finished the lap.

Nothing happened.

I waited. Still nothing.

I raised my hands questioningly toward Charlie.

He, between chuckles, managed to call out, "Rooster! Rooster!"

I rolled my eyes and crowed like a rooster.

-*"It makes sense."*
-*"Don't mock me. The leprechaun did enough of that."*

*

But then something did happen.

The whole tree started moving and rustling. One of the branches shot out, jamming itself straight ahead, deep into my chest.

I froze in place, more surprised than hurt. I tried to scream, but I was only able to gurgle. I held the hard bark of the branch with both hands, trying to pull it out. With everything I had. And I had lots of strength.

But the branch only dug deeper into my body. Beyond it, I could feel - again, pain-free - how cold little roots came out of it. They grew and branched out inside my body, into my arms, legs, stomach, and head. I felt nauseous. I didn't want to move.

Then the next stage started. The tree began pulsating steadily, sending the beat into my body through the branch. Every pulse was a memory. A moment. An emotion, information, another piece of myself.

With every pulse, the tree shriveled. A wave of frozen, electric power surged into me from the outside and paralyzed me, drowning me in my own memories. Luckily it didn't take long. Maybe twenty pulses, maybe less. The tree deepened its grip on me, growing further into my body, losing its physical presence. Everything shriveled: branches, leaves, roots.

There were other things invading me. The tree wasn't made out of memories alone. New secrets were encrypted inside it.

My knees went weak, but I couldn't fall down. The branch was lodged deep in my chest, holding me upright. Out of the corner of my eye, I saw the leprechaun still sitting on the rock. He was no longer laughing, just looking at me, astonished.

"Help me," I gurgled at him.

But he didn't move. What could he have done?

I kept trying to pull the branch out of myself by force, but I couldn't even make it budge. The tree kept flowing into me, filling me up. Eventually, it uprooted itself entirely and gathered itself completely into the branch, coming into me as a whole and then

126

disappearing.

I fell to my knees, petrified. I couldn't even breathe. In a way, it was like my awakening moment in Heaven, minus the pain. But the helplessness, the stagnation, the paralysis… all those were present.

"Are you okay, Master?"

The leprechaun leaned over me, his brows furrowed with concern. I started feeling better. Much better, actually. Slowly, the cold sensation faded away, leaving behind another feeling. A better one. Like the feeling you get after a hard workout. The kind that leaves you tired, with exhausted muscles, but with a sense of accomplishment.

*

"You can come out now," I called.

A rustle behind the bushes told me M was not far away. She must have witnessed the whole thing. I know if I was her, I would definitely have hidden close by and watched. After a few seconds, she stepped out from the bushes, treading carefully. Her forehead was wrinkled with concern.

"Are you feeling okay?"

"I've never felt better," I half lied. I could feel how the tree was continuing to assimilate itself into me. It hurt a little, but also felt good, a light, high feeling, growing stronger. The process, I knew, was about to change me dramatically. I think she knew that, too.

"The tree's gone." She pointed to the place it had been up until a few moments ago.

"Yes. Have you ever seen anything like that?"

"Heaven is a big place. I've seen a lot of things."

She waited for me to tell her what had happened. But I was too busy with myself and what I had just experienced to share. She waited, and the silence grew. Her eyes scanned me from top to bottom, especially my chest area, the place where the branch had speared into me. I felt around it. There wasn't even a sign of a scar. The silence lengthened.

"Is there something I need to know?" she eventually asked.

"Is there something you want to know?"

She took a deep breath, like she was going to start saying something long and important, but then stopped. A wrinkle of worry appeared on her forehead and she tilted her head to listen.

I heard it too. A familiar, distant hum. M tensed up. Charlie jumped into the bushes and disappeared. I still felt a little high, trying to locate the direction of the sound. I couldn't, and then after a second I understood why.

It was coming from all directions.

BATTLE

"Is that...?"

"Mmhmm," she answered. "Run."

But I couldn't move. I didn't want to. I kept listening, looking around, trying to anticipate where the attack would come from. M did exactly the same thing, but then she noticed I was still next to her.

She turned on her heels and looked at me with a grave face. "Run! Beam out!"

"No, I don't think so." I closed my hands into fists. Would they do any good? I had to know. My heart started pounding wildly, rivers of adrenaline flowing into my bloodstream. The tree in me moved. I felt new things awaken within me. New powers.

*

-*"Why didn't you run away?"*
-*"I don't know. Maybe I'd gotten tired of running."*

*

With two quick steps, M was standing in front of me, screaming at me nose to nose.

"Get the hell out of here! Don't you understand you have to?"

Her eyes narrowed, shooting daggers, saliva spraying out of her mouth into mine. I didn't waver. Her closeness was rather nice. The humming grew louder, but the body heat she was radiating eliminated all sense of danger. Suddenly I had to touch her, envelop her...

A sharp slap woke me up.

"Idiot child! This is what I've worked so hard for? Get out of here! Beam! Run!"

And then they arrived. The first swarm of pixies came directly behind her, shooting out of the tree line with an angry buzz and sparkling eyes. M turned toward them in panic and then waved her hands wildly at them as if to signal them to stay away. It didn't help. The pixies went right through her, on a direct route to me. Almost

200 of them.

I lifted my hand toward them. I had intended to just punch the center of the swarm and cause as much damage as I could, but the result was completely different. A sort of shock wave came out of my hand and vibrated through the air at a low frequency. The wave hit the center of the swarm, like a truck hitting a flock of pigeons that haven't flown out of the street in time. A cloud of yellow pixies was tossed far out into the jungle. I could hear trees splinter, bones shatter, wings break, and little squeaks of pain.

M looked at me, her jaw hanging open.

I was surprised myself. But only for a fraction of a second, because instantly another two swarms attacked me, humming furiously. Each one of them got a wave of my hand, one after the other. The shock waves that came from it this time were more powerful. They twisted the air, like the waves that emanate from a blazing fire. This time, the results were much more destructive. Some of the pixies flew out of sight, but the majority just disintegrated into dust, which was then scattered by the wind.

For a few moments there was silence in the jungle. Was that all?

I glanced at M. The surprised look on her face turned into a smile of satisfaction. She nodded her head lightly, as if she was congratulating me on my new powers. Then another sharp hum filled the air, and another swarm of pixies went past her on their way to me.

I tensed up and waved my hand to take care of them. But I didn't have to. With an experienced and decisive motion, M lifted her palm up and then slammed it down quickly.

I felt the ground shake from the shock wave. Not just me: all the pixies that went by her slammed into the ground, like mosquitos being smacked with a fly swatter. Some broke apart on impact, some shattered to pieces, some just got buried in the softer patches of dirt.

Now it was my turn to stand in awe, mouth agape. How did she do that? And if she could do that, why hadn't she done it before? But I didn't have time to ask many questions. A new wave of attackers came, hundreds of pixies simultaneously. Maybe more. From all directions. Swarms over swarms, mostly toward me, but some swarmed M as well.

They didn't stand a chance. She moved both her hands in an elaborate Tai Chi motion and a ring of fire erupted from her body and blasted around her. I felt the air burning around me. The pixies felt it more. They melted in the air and dripped onto the ground.

I had another idea. When the next swarm attacked me, I swirled my finger around quickly. A little cyclone formed right above me and started sucking in every little stinging creature that tried to come near me. They disappeared into it with meek screams.

Finally, I allowed myself to smile. The first adrenaline wave set in. I was invincible.

More swarms came, drowning the forest with all kinds of colors and a loud hum. But none of the pixies managed to even come near us. M and I, in movements that became more and more synchronized, destroyed them all, almost dancing while we did it. It was fun.

We started to vary our methods. We incinerated them once while they were moving, and another time we slammed two swarms into each other, crashing them against their friends. A flash of knowledge told me I could create a sort of black hole in space, which would suck in everyone around it. When a new wave of swarms came at us, I unleashed a few rounds like that. I bought us a few seconds of silence.

"Where are they coming from?" I asked.

"More importantly..." she panted, "... why now?"

I thought I knew the answer. But before I had a chance to guess, I heard a rustling noise. Not a hum, but a sort of rustle coming from the ground. M furrowed her brows and looked around quickly, trying to find out where they would come from next.

"What now?" I asked.

"Thunder rats," she said.

*

-"*Actual rats?*"

-"*Of course not. But whoever designed them must have based them on the real thing. Their fur was made out of shiny, needle-sharp hairs. And they had yellow vampire fangs, narrow eyes, and a cry like rolling thunder. They didn't have tails and they ran insanely fast.*"

*

I froze them in the air. Literally. I did that with a kick and an ice-cold stare. They were still a few feet away from me, mid-charge, with

131

foul drool dripping from their fangs. Then the kick pulled them all up into the air and turned them into ice blocks.

When they fell back to the ground, each one shattered into thousands of smoking and bleeding fragments.

M, on her side, settled for shock waves. I could use them as well, just as effectively. But I wanted more. I wanted to find more and more things. Thinking back, that was a mistake.

Unlike the pixies, the rats did not come as a coordinated swarm. They charged us more like an angry mob of individuals, each one picking a course and a target for itself. That made them a little less predictable and a little harder to neutralize, but still, the fact that they all charged me helped; a step forward, a backhand wave, a swirl in a circle...

And then I saw him, leaning lazily over against of the trees.

A living statue of muscles, with skin the shade of lightning and eyes made of flame. Rage, I remembered. The closest thing to God here. The one Duke was so afraid of. The one who surfed the largest wave in the universe, and I had been sure he hadn't given me a moment of attention.

Well, now I was his center of attention. His lips were stretched in a light smile and his hands were joined across his pecs in a demonstrative manner. He didn't make a conscious effort to join the battle, but from behind his legs came a herd of thunder rats. They charged us again.

"Do you know who that is?" I asked M and pointed to Rage, while I turned those predatory pouncing beasts into a screaming herd of whispering embers.

She looked. Her eyes narrowed.

"Trouble."

She burned another row of thunder rats, then knelt toward Rage and made a sharp, indecent movement. A bundle of blue pulsating balls of light shot out of her hands. A massive explosion deafened me.

For a moment the whole world burned in blue flames, then went back to the regular colors. The destruction was massive. Within a radius of several yards from the center of the explosion, nothing was left. Not trees, not bushes, not grass. Rage was gone too. For a second I thought she had blown him up, but then I heard something else. A different kind of humming. Not as sharp and squawky as the pixies. Lower, powerful. Impressive.

Above the tree line rose a large dragonfly. Over sixty-six feet of predatory nightmare, blue and shimmering. It was propelled by four transparent wings double that length, fluttering at a dizzying speed. At the front of its head were two monstrous eyes, each one the size of a car, made out of hundreds of little hexagonal mirrors. Not far below them were two sharp, black jaws, each one about fifteen feet long. Immediately I remembered I had seen them before. I had seen them when I was surfing the rainbow and had the vision of José Johnson, trapped. At the time, I'd thought I was hallucinating. Clearly, I must not have been.

At the end of the dragonfly's tail was a menacing, twinkling red stinger swaying from side to side. On its back sat Rage. He appeared very relaxed. The smile was still on his lips. The dragonfly closed its jaws and opened them again. The sound was like a pair of very sharp scissors.

For the first time that day, I tasted fear. I balled my hands into fists. I knew there was a lot more power hiding inside me, many abilities I had yet to discover. Somewhere inside me existed a solution to this monster, too. But would I be able to find it in time? I hesitated.

A line of blue energy balls whistled past me from behind. M, apparently, did not hesitate. The balls cut through space on their way to the dragonfly, but it rose higher and the balls missed. They disappeared into the horizon without exploding.

Now it was the dragonfly's turn to react. It opened its jaws a little and shot a shining beam of orange plasma.

It burned. A lot. I felt my skin sear and crack, and I fell to my knees, protecting my head with my hands. The orange beam enveloped me, sticking to me. I felt helpless. Completely lost. I was already welcoming my return to the white awakening room, but then the burning stopped as suddenly as it had started.

A cool breeze caressed my body. Soothing, healing. Cooling. It had a familiar smell. What was it? A smell directly related to my memory. I knew it. But I couldn't remember what it was. Odd thoughts to have while battling a giant dragonfly.

"Get up, get up!" I heard M screaming, straining.

I spared a glance her way and was thrilled by what I saw. She stood there like an old holo superhero, with her feet shoulder-width apart, planted firmly on the ground, every muscle in her body vibrating from the effort. Her right hand had created a shield made of wind that pushed the orange beam aside. Her left hand sent a green, soothing flow to me. Aloe Vera, I realized.

Rage and his dragonfly changed their angle and aimed at her.

I couldn't leave her alone in the fight. I got up at once and started generating a massive amount of energy in my arms. It was completely by instinct, unexplainable. I felt it pulsating, and then I released it in the direction of the dragonfly.

The intensity of the blast made M's energy balls look like popcorn popping.

The world flickered for a moment in shades of red, orange, and yellow. Deafening thunder roared from every direction.

If someone had been observing from the side, I would guess it would have appeared that a golden half-moon came out of me and split the dragonfly in half. I saw the two pieces falling to the ground. Each one of them kept moving like there was still life in it. Its jaws landed next to me. Up close they were even more impressive. It was truly a monster.

Rage was nowhere to be seen. He had probably escaped before it hit him, I guessed.

And I was right.

Above the tree line a new dragonfly rose. After it, another one. And many more.

M and I looked at each other.

"You should have run when I told you to," she said.

*

-*"How long did it last?"*
-*"I don't remember. Maybe an hour? Maybe more. A long time, a lot of energy. A lot of effort."*

*

As the battle wore on, the world moved faster and faster. I turned right. I turned left. I turned around. One of the dragonflies was just above me, with an evil look in its eyes and jaws wide open. Only in the last fraction of a second did I succeed in pushing it away and smashing it into one of the trees.

Another attack came from the left, too fast for me. M blocked it, but the distraction cost her dearly. A beam of plasma scorched her entire body and she screamed. I smelled seared flesh. Even the smell came too fast.

And then I understood what was happening.

There was too much action around me. Too much information. Too many memories. No matter what new powers I had, I had become too slow to use them. I blew up a swarm of pixies that pounced on my legs, then rolled out of the clearing to look for cover. My movements were so slow, so tired...

Why was this happening? It wasn't long ago that I had uploaded into the rainbow waterfall. I wasn't supposed to be so loaded down; I wasn't supposed to be so tired...

I tried to beam, but I couldn't.

*

-*"Hah! Your power's limited?"*

-*"Exactly. All this commotion around me, it cost me energy. I had special powers, but they were only effective for a limited time, until my energy was depleted, and then I needed a power pack to reload.*

-*"Did you have a power pack?"*

-*"No."*

*

I started laughing loudly, sounding very slow to my ears. A swarm of pixies jumped on my face and started gnawing at my eyes, but I kept laughing, ignoring the pain. My stomach shook with laughter. Two dragonflies spit fire at me, turning me into a burning, scorching inferno, and still I kept laughing.

I felt my hands melt, my legs break. The pain was horrible, almost as bad as my awakening moments in Heaven, but I just couldn't stop laughing. I had always loved a good joke, even if it was at my expense. Even if it was on me.

I think I was screaming with laughter all the way to the end.

PRISON

A white light shone through my eyelids.

I moaned in pain. I tried to move but couldn't. I hadn't thought I would succeed. My experiences in the awakening room had taught me that there's very little you can do right after you wake up. Still, the sensation was different from the previous times. True, my body was sore, but not as much. In fact, the pain was more like a sunburn after too many hours at the beach. It was external pain.

The light was not the same light. Even with my eyes closed I could make out shadows and shapes. There was nothing that reminded me of the white room. From a distance, I could hear faint sounds. Mumbles, screams, shrieks.

I opened my eyes at once.

*

-*"That sounds different from a regular awakening."*
-*"True. And it was the second time I'd been scared. There's something calming in the knowledge that you can't die. Or more so, that death is only the beginning of a new round. There's something scary about knowing you survived."*

*

I really wasn't in a white room.

It was transparent. A little cell made out of crystalline glass, cold and hard. I was on my back, with a sore head and a stiff neck. I turned my head slowly. To my right I could see thick glass bars, and beyond them was a glass corridor lit by a white light.

I rolled onto my stomach and tried to lift myself up. I paid a heavy price for that with pain. My head was pounding like someone had beaten it with a bat. I guess that was sort of what had happened. My cheeks were burning. My muscles ached. But I didn't give up. With a lot of effort, I managed to get up on my elbows and after that, onto my hands. I switched to sitting and carefully scoped out my surroundings.

I was in a jail cell. That was obvious. It wasn't big, about half the

136

size of my old room at my mother's house. But it had no furniture; it had nothing in it at all. Everything around me was glass. Completely transparent, going on for miles in each direction. Miles of similar jail cells, some empty, some inhabited by prisoners like me.

I looked up. My glass ceiling was another cell's floor, where a gorgeous redhead lay on her back. Her ass, back, and feet were lying flattened right over my head. On the floor above that were the large feet of a green man. Above him were a few empty cells, and above those were more prisoners, one to each cell. In the cell to my right was a man with Asian features, tall and bald. He was practicing some sort of meditation. In the cell to my left was a plump and ample woman.

Unlike the youthful look that most people in Heaven chose, this woman looked much older. She was still quite attractive, but the impressive detail she sported was a large tattoo of the stars and stripes, the American flag, the version with fifty-two stars.

She waved at me. I waved back.

"Hey," I said.

She shook her head and pointed to her ears. She couldn't hear anything.

"Hey!" I yelled, but she shook her head again sadly. Yelling probably wouldn't help me.

I tried sharing my thoughts. Nothing happened. Something in the glass must have blocked the ability to communicate between cells. Still, the silence wasn't complete. From the corridor, voices came constantly, one of them familiar. It was M's voice. She was screaming in pain. Screaming loudly.

I walked over to the bars and tried to bend them. That failed, of course. I hadn't thought they would bend so easily. I tried to crack them by all kinds of methods, even break them with my fists, but when that became too painful I had to stop. The screaming had stopped for the moment, and I wondered where M was. I hoped she'd managed to escape. I tried to convince myself that she was more experienced than I was and had surely gotten out. I looked for her among the transparent cells, but the prison was huge. Indeed, I was surrounded by walls of people in thousands of cells. I couldn't see her, but maybe she was being kept in a cell far from me. Or hidden from me in some other way.

Time passed.

Slowly I healed. The burns healed. The soreness in my body

ceased. And the tiredness, the biggest curse, passed too.

And if I wasn't tired, then I could…

*

-"Did you get out?"
-"No. Apparently I couldn't use any special abilities. Or beam. Those glass cells functioned perfectly."

*

"Hey!" I screamed through the bars.

No one answered.

"Heeeyyyy!" I screamed again. And again. And again.

After I had screamed 24,574 times (I counted), someone came. It was the mayor, or a comparable AI. He even brought the chair and a suitcase. He eyed me, nodded, and sat down in front of me. For a few hours he looked at me, and then at his open suitcase, then at me again. I swore to myself that the moment I got out, I would blow him up again. To illustrate my intent, I started screaming at him, punching the glass bars with all my might right in front of him. He didn't even blink.

For weeks after, my hand hurt. I had no doubt I had broken my fingers. Outside of the prison, this crystal wasn't bad: every blow healed within minutes or hours. Inside the prison, it was a whole different story, much like the world I had left downstairs.

Eventually, I stopped screaming. I started losing my sense of time. It was horrible. I wasn't given food or drink, but I didn't need them to survive. On the other hand, the hunger and thirst were there and were horrific. I couldn't turn them off. I couldn't switch the loneliness off either. I was surrounded by people in all directions and I couldn't communicate with them. Even the information from the Pedia was denied me. It drove me insane.

It drove me insane.

Every now and then, I heard screaming from one direction or another. Masculine screams, feminine screams. There were echoes of screams and explosions. More screaming and more crying. I could never see who was doing the screaming. Even though the prison was transparent, I didn't see the action itself. But every now and then, I saw lightning reflected off the crystal walls. It usually appeared when the screaming began.

I heard M once more. It was a long time later. Her first scream sounded familiar, but after a while I was sure it was her. And she cried, and she yelled, and she screamed, and she was in pain as if they were tearing her limbs off one by one. I could almost feel it myself. I felt helpless. There was nothing I could do but shout her name and try to get my body through those transparent walls. I ran from side to side and slammed myself against them. I screamed. I wept. I raged.

Around me, left and right, up and down, people noticed and looked at me with pity.

For me or for them, I will never know. Probably for everyone.

*

Then he came to me.

I didn't see when and how it happened. I was busy trying to see as far as I could through the walls of people around me. I tried to locate M. When I finally turned around, he was suddenly just there, looking at me from the other side of the bars. I jumped back. It was the first time I had had a chance to see him up close. He was very big, muscular, lit with a restless, inner electric current. His eyes were simply balls of flames. You couldn't look at them. Next to him, I must have looked like a lump of coal.

I thought he would interrogate me from the outside. But he walked in. Through the bars. Literally, through the bars. He just went through them as if they were made of air.

"Who am I?" he asked after he entered. His voice was soft and calm. His eyes blinded me.

"You're Rage."

"And who are you?"

"Royal. Royal Black."

His presence was paralyzing. He came closer and I could feel how my strength was being sucked out of me, leaving my body. I swayed, leaned against the wall, and eventually had to collapse and sit. He kept moving closer and eventually stood almost on top of me. His hands clasped across his chest, his bare feet in a wide stance, he was the picture of dominance. My head was as high as his pelvis. I guessed he was probably aware of that.

"We have no file on Royal Black. You don't exist."

"If I don't exist, then set me free."

139

Rage exhaled and from his pelvic area a painful lightning bolt shot straight into my eye. From there it went through my entire body, not skipping a single organ. It didn't hurt. It was much more than just pain.

I found myself on the floor, twitching. My body still had currents jolting through it, biting constantly. I wanted to die.

"Why... why did you do that?" I eventually gurgled.

"Because I don't have time for you, Newborn. Either you tell me how you got here, or you'll be sorry for the moment you did."

I took it upon myself to take a moment to recuperate. And to think. For some reason, Rage assumed I was Newborn, but why? Were there other Newborn here?

I pulled myself up off the floor and sat down again. "I am not Newborn," I said quietly, preparing myself for another dose of pain.

But it didn't come. Rage, it seemed, was open to listening. That was good.

"So, who are you?"

I saw no reason to lie. "Like I said, I'm Royal Black. But, but!" I quickly added before he struck me with another bolt of lightning. "When I was downstairs, they called me Roy Schwartz."

In retrospect, I've no doubt that I confessed too quickly. To expose my true identity, after what I had done to the system downstairs, was surely a recipe for heavy punishment. But I was completely broken. I hadn't spoken to anyone in so long and with the terrible pain surging through my body, the thirst and the hunger... and above all, knowing that it would go on forever... I think I just wanted to die. Die for good.

Rage tilted his head as if he was checking something. After a second he looked down at me. What he said was the absolute last thing I expected.

"You are not Roy Schwartz."

*

-*"What?"*
-*"Yep."*

*

"I am! I hacked into Heaven thirty years ago and -"

140

Another jolt of electricity stopped me. This time it was more powerful. More painful. It left me twitching for longer than before. But it did not prevent me from listening and Rage knew it.

"You are not Roy Schwartz." He started a long and confusing lecture. "And couldn't be Roy Schwartz, either. Obviously, you are Newborn. It's unclear how you uploaded without identification, so listen to me: up until now, I've managed to catch every operative of yours. Are you listening? Every one of your agents. They're all here! And none of them will ever get out of here. Ever! And neither will you. And when I say 'never,' I mean it. Heaven has existed for a long time and will always exist. That's a fact. And you, the Newborn, refuse to accept it! You and your pathetic attempts to get in here. So who are you? And how did you get here?"

He kept going like that, on and on. The man just loved hearing himself talk.

But more than he liked hearing himself, he loved zapping me. It went on for hours. Maybe days. I don't remember. I do remember pain, and screams, and the hard floor. And the hopelessness I felt against his power. He really was the closest thing to God Heaven had. But as God, he had to get the truth.

And he just didn't believe it.

*

I didn't see when and how he left the cell.

My eyes were watering. The physical pain was almost unbearable, but it was a distant second to the absolute knowledge that I would never, ever get out of there. I was condemned to a life of torture, an eternity of hopelessness. There was nothing I could do. There was no hope. I knew Rage would zap me, melt me, vaporize me, and crush me any time his sadistic soul desired. Then he would pick me up again and forget me in this tiny, impenetrable glass room until the next time.

Even worse, I suspected that until that time arrived, I would miss it. Maybe wait a whole year for it. Maybe a decade. Maybe a thousand years. In a place where time has no meaning, there is no meaning to life. And the only way this nightmare would end was if Heaven was destroyed. Gone. Suddenly the thought that the Newborn might tear the place down didn't seem so bad. It would mean the absolute and immediate disappearance of Heaven. If that happened, then what was the point? I would never know about it. I would just... stop being.

I think I cried, really cried, for days on end. No one came to me, no one talked to me. The lady with the stars and stripes tattoo tried to calm me down, I think. She looked at me a little, tried to wave her hands, but eventually gave up. Afterwards, I started hearing M's screams, out there. He was probably interrogating her about me. That didn't make anything better.

I found myself sitting on the floor, in the corner, staring at the bars.

Thick, round, unwavering. Like bent lenses, they distorted what was happening in the hallway. The transparent cells, the people rotting in them. The white light. Then suddenly, one of them looked different.

My heart skipped a beat.

MEMORY 11

The mist came, the mist went away.

I was invisible, floating over Heaven's landscape. It was after I had sent Mom to Heaven. I had already hidden the invincibility packet inside the tree in the jungle, and now I was looking for another place to hide Heaven's core code. I didn't know where to put it. It was a massive code; it had sequences that in time would have been found, no doubt. I couldn't just hide it in another tree, or underground, or on the moon; it would stick out like fireworks at night.

No, I had to hide it in some other way. Somewhere it wouldn't stick out. Somewhere no one would think to look for it and no one would happen upon it. It had to be a place I would surely go to at some point. But not immediately. Not before I found out who I was and how I had even gotten into Heaven.

Where the hell could I hide that code?

And then I saw the crystal prison. It shimmered, as it always did, next to the needle tower, where no ordinary man could go. I had passed by it a few times before and always told myself if I made it to Heaven, then I would probably eventually find myself there. It had tens of thousands of cells, but very few people imprisoned by its dense firewall. I wondered what had brought them there. And when, if ever, they would be set free.

The existence of a prison in Heaven was a mystery. Why was it necessary?

To make it impenetrable, the walls of the prison were programs straight out of the core code. They didn't obey any of the rules in Heaven and were designed so that it would be almost impossible to crack them. Meaning, if I added something to them, no one would notice.

If I could have smiled, I would have. I had found it. Yes, yes, I had found it. I hovered toward the prison and fought the urge to free everyone locked in it just to piss off the system. I didn't do it, of course. Why draw needless attention?

I landed on the roof and unloaded the access code. At the last moment, just for fun, I added my signature to it.

The mist came.

SHATTERING

It was Charlie.

The leprechaun. He hid very close to the bottom of the bars, looking me straight in the eyes. It was obvious he wasn't in one of the cells, but actually inside the crystal bar itself. Behind him was a different background, golden. Charlie smiled, bounced a gold coin, and went back into hiding.

I suddenly stood up.

The bar went back to looking like the others, completely transparent. Maybe I was imagining it? Maybe it was because of the angle I was looking at it? I leaned back against the side of the cell and slowly slid down. Only when I had slipped all the way down, when my butt touched the ground, did Charlie reappear. He looked straight into my eyes again, smiled again, bounced a gold coin again, then went back to hiding inside the rod.

I looked around, then up and down. None of my neighbors noticed me or my behavior. And what had I really done, anyway? Gotten up and sat back down? There was no reason for them to notice it. And yet I was concerned.

Slowly I went close to the bar and 'accidentally' touched it. I didn't want to draw needless attention. I just leaned back against the wall, trying to hide my hand touching the bar where Charlie hid. The one with the core code. The feeling was similar to the one I had felt when the tree flowed into me. A frigid transfusion, streaming into my body from within the bar. The intensity grew and built up inside of me. I tasted it, relishing every terabyte that flowed into me. Slowly, the constant pain disappeared. Slowly, I started breathing deeply.

Relaxed, I let the code pour into me for a few long minutes. The place where I touched the bar glowed. I hoped no one would pass by right now, and I wiggled my fingers. The bar that, until a few minutes ago had been stiff and unbreakable, succumbed to them like jelly. I could have left right at that moment, but I waited. I had patience and the core code was very big.

I closed my eyes.

I imagined myself floating over my own body. And then that was really where I was. Black, strong, leaning against the bars, with all the muscles in my body vibrating. A feeling of déjà vu took me over. This was exactly how I had seen Heaven some thirty years ago, when I hacked into it and hovered around in it. Seeing but unseen.

I extended my range of vision in all directions. More and more people came into view. Hundreds of people. I could see them, trapped in their cells, hungry, thirsty, hurting. Some paced from side to side. Some were curled up in the fetal position. Suddenly, I saw the Buddhist monk from Midlake. His orange robe was torn, his yellow face broken and bruised. Other people just sat and stared into space. One of them caught my attention.

It was José. He was injured all over, his cheetah fur marked with what looked like lashes from a whip. His nose was missing. When I looked closer, I saw his teeth were missing. I could feel his pain, thick and burning. But more than that, I could sense his concern. Concern for Jackie. Where was she, anyway?

"She escaped." His voice echoed in my ears without him moving his lips.

"Hold on," I whispered. "I'm close."

His eyes were shut, but under his lids, his eyes started moving. I knew he could hear me. I tried to send him positive feelings. I hoped they reached him.

I moved away from him and expanded my mind further. Hundreds more people came into it. None of them was Jackie.

But one of them was M.

Her cell was different from the rest. Unlike the smooth, crystal floors of the other cells, – hers was made out of sharp needles. She lay on them, trying to divide her weight over as much of the surface as she could. Still, they were sharp enough to injure her. Thousands of needles, each one an inch long, stabbed her. They were red from clotted blood. On some of them the blood was still dripping.

M was lying on her back, but the front of her body looked like a bleeding strainer. She must have turned every now and then. Her eyes were closed tightly. Something inside me wrenched in pain.

I came closer to her, and she opened her eyes and looked straight at me.

"Save me," she whispered through parched lips.

*

I opened my eyes inside my cell.

145

The bar I held on to glowed with a bright, white glare. Wave after wave of energy flowed into it from the walls, and from it into me. I took a deep breath and opened myself to receive the core code, completely and instantly.

For a moment I felt like a massive waterfall was rushing over my head. The noise from the information smashing into me was tremendous, drowning out any external sound. It didn't hurt, it didn't make me uncomfortable. It was just like sitting at the bottom of Niagara Falls with thousands of tons of water crashing over my head every second. And pouring into me.

My vision was foggy as well. The corridor, the cell, and the people next to me - they all blurred into shadows of light in a world made of burning crystal. My skin was freezing cold. Inside my blood boiled. And all of it, painless. No suffering. Just the complete flooding of my senses, my arteries, of all the...

"Save me," I heard her whisper to me again, with more intensity than any scream.

Out of rage, I clenched the hand holding the bar.

It shattered.

And following that, the entire glass prison.

Floors upon floors of unbreakable prison, unpliable, became a din of breaking glass. The sound of a million glasses shattering could be heard in every direction. And after it, screams. Thousands of hopeless, broken people falling to the ground all at once as the floor underneath them disappeared. Including me. My cell was about three hundred feet up. I fell hard.

I landed on a mountain of bodies and crystalline dust. Soon I became part of the mountain, as I was buried under more and more people falling onto me and it. At first it only hurt a little—an elbow in my eye, a knee in my stomach—but as the layer of people above me became buried in turn, I felt the increasing weight pressing down on me. The sound of breaking glass slowly subsided and left a relative silence punctuated by the dim sounds of bodies colliding. Those sounds faded, too, the more bodies stacked up on top of me.

I had never been buried inside a mountain of people and glass dust. It was an interesting feeling, very sensual. The touch, for the most part, was nice. I figured I'd have to try it again under more pleasant conditions. But in the meantime, I had to get out.

I tried to move, but the weight of the bodies was too great. I thought about beaming out, but a large thigh was covering my eyes and I didn't want to find myself stuck in some tree or the belly of a mountain. I didn't know what would happen in such a situation. On the other hand, I remembered that the prison was next to the needle tower, and both were surrounded by miles of open fields. So I took a chance and beamed three hundred feet forward.

I beamed out.

I found myself in the air and immediately fell down to the ground on my side. A very sharp pain alerted me that I had broken my hand, but magically, it started to re-form, healing almost instantly. I groaned with both pain and happiness. Outside the crystal prison, my healing powers were back!

I looked at the place where I had landed. A soft, well-trimmed lawn, fenced by a fragrant row of red rose bushes. The sun was shining happily, a liquid marble statue danced to its light, mixing and forming new, harmonious shapes at every moment. The air was filled with a harp's melody, but a stronger noise drowned it out: thousands of people moaning in pain.

I turned around and looked at the shimmering mountain of bodies. It was quickly shrinking as more and more people understood they could, finally, beam away and escape. Within seconds there were only a few dozen people, semi-buried in a large pile of shining crystal dust. Where was M? At first I didn't see her, and I hoped she had gotten away, although, in her condition, I wasn't sure she was even able to.

And then I saw a pale hand stained with smeared blood reaching out of the hill of dust. That hand felt about and was then joined by another hand; with weak motions she started extricating herself from the pile.

I tried to get up, but couldn't. My body couldn't yet contain the power surging through it. The sensation was much more powerful than what I had felt when the tree was flowing into me. Everything was roiling inside and I couldn't contain it. I couldn't control my limbs. My muscles were quivering and I had to wait for them to stop.

But I didn't have time. I imagined the sound of the crystal prison shattering had been heard throughout Heaven. I was certain Rage would arrive shortly.

I was right.

He beamed there with a thud. A real thud. When he landed, the ground shook. He was taller, more muscular, and bigger than I remembered. About thirteen feet tall. Around his body was a lightning storm. A real one. His eyes were like floodlights.

I understood why his name was Rage, and I prepared myself for his attack. But when his flaming gaze focused on me, I still couldn't get up. I lay on the grass like a giant slug, twisting and twitching in waves. I expected to feel his full strength hit me any minute.

But I was wrong. He kept looking for something and eventually stopped when he spied the top of the hill of shimmering crystal shards.

"You!" he thundered. His voice echoed again and again as if we were inside a little valley in the mountains and not on an open plain. "You!"

With one leap, he jumped and landed next to M. Only her upper body was exposed; Rage grabbed her arm and with a limb-ripping yank pulled her up and out like a rag doll.

I watched in horror how her fragile, pale body spiraled up, out of control, a quarter of a mile into the air. She flipped back and forth, starting to come down, and then something happened. A wave of light formed around her body, and suddenly M looked completely healthy. No bruises, no scratches; totally fine.

She paused in midair, a few dozen feet up, and levitated.

"You," she said in a quiet voice that somehow carried across the distance. Then she shot forward, flying directly toward Rage, pulling her feet up to kick him.

They clashed with a crackling sound, flying together into the hill of crystal dust and sinking into it. I couldn't see what was going on under the hill, but it started pulsing with light, as if a full-blown electrical storm was raging inside. Every now and then, shards of glass flew out of it, and every few seconds muffled sounds of pain could be heard. Both female and male.

I tried to get to my feet, this time with more success. Slowly, I regained control of my basic motor skills. I was still shaking, but managed to walk a few steps forward, when all at once Rage flew out of the hill and rolled onto the ground right next to me.

He looked bruised and beaten, covered in blood. His stomach was punctured. I couldn't believe my eyes. A few seconds later, M crawled out of the hill. She wasn't in much better shape. She hopped on one leg, the other one twisted at an impossible angle. Rage started to pick himself up off the ground, but M had both her hands aimed at him and out of them came blue balls of light. The first barrage hit the mark, but didn't damage Rage sufficiently. He blocked the rest with his right hand, and with his left he made a fist and slammed it into the ground.

Out of the ground under M's legs, a pointed, metal pole erupted. It skewered her right hand, and I heard bone cracking and pale skin ripping apart.

M screamed and tried to pull her right hand away using her left. Her attack stopped.

Then it was Rage's turn. He had barely gotten to his feet when he opened his mouth for a roar that turned into a jet of fire. A thin, focused, and brutal jet, slowly made its way toward the trapped M and then blew up in her face. The smell of scorched flesh filled the air. She fell to the ground, flames dancing around her. The skewer was still lodged deep in her hand.

Rage slowly started walking toward her, step by step. The ground shook under him again, and I saw how the wounds on his body were healing with each step he took. Next to him, out of thin air, a long broadsword appeared, burning with purple flames. It was like something out of a legend, even bigger than he was. But he carried it easily and made his way toward what was left of M.

She tried to escape, but couldn't.

All she could do was turn one blue eye to me and whisper, "Help me. The core..."

*

-*"In the old movies, before the holos, this would be the time for the hero to scream 'Nooooooo!' and then trash the villain up."*
-*"And you didn't scream?"*
-*"No. I really wanted to win."*

*

The core code was in me, filling me with new powers. But I still couldn't attack Rage. I was too weak and I hadn't realized at all what I could do. But M, it seemed, did know. And asked for it.

I tried not to think too much. I sent a vein of energy out of my body to M. It came from my heart, symbolic, flowing quickly into her body. Straight through her bellybutton. Her center mass.

The effect was immediate.

I felt a mighty surge of energy from me to her. The vein pulsated and flickered quickly. I fell to my knees, drained, black spots dancing in front of my eyes. Even though I tried to focus, I couldn't see what was happening. All I heard were the sounds of a struggle, screams of pain, and eventually panting and muffled voices.

When I managed to open my eyes, the battle had ended. The first thing I saw was a hundred feet to my right: a perfect, transparent crystal pyramid, sixty feet high, twinkling with a reddish hue. Inside it, like a fossilized insect inside a piece of amber, was Rage. He had been completely frozen, mid-motion, and only the lightning under his skin kept moving. For the first time since I had met him, his eyes were extinguished. Instead of fireballs, they were just regular, brown eyes.

He moved his eyes and looked at me. "You're making a mistake," I heard him think at me.

Then the Earth opened under the crystal pyramid, and it dropped downward with a thud.

The ground closed back up over it.

*

The sun was shining. Birds were chirping.

In the distance I could hear honey bees suck nectar from the rose bushes. Everything was finally quiet. Pastoral and quiet. From my heart, the artery of life was steadily sending the core code of Heaven to my woman. The woman who had saved my life. The woman who had come out victorious over the closest thing to God.

She got to her feet. She was injured, cut, bleeding everywhere. The right side of her face was burned down to the bone. Her right hand was hanging by threads of ripped skin. She looked the worst I had ever seen her. But she was alive, and we were free, and Heaven was waiting for us. For good.

"I love you," I said shakily. With great effort, I got up to go to her.

"I know. I'm sorry."

CORE

-*"WTT?"*
-*"Shut up and listen."*

*

For a moment I didn't know what to say. And then it hit me. She hit me.

She lifted her good hand and out of it shot energy balls. Just like those that had hit Rage earlier. They had barely affected him, but they wrecked me. They hurt my stomach, chest, and head, exploding all over me.

I fell back, almost completely paralyzed. I could only move my left hand, and with it I tried to pull the artery of life out of myself. I couldn't. It was just like my attempt to pull the tree branch out of me. Physical strength wasn't enough, and I didn't have a lot of strength anyway. After a second I couldn't move my left hand either. The grass on which I lay lengthened, twisted, and tied my hands and legs down. Its grip tightened and I was pinned to the ground. Another blade twisted itself around my throat.

I moaned. The umbilical cord kept steadily sucking energy out of me. It drained not only the core code out of me, but all of me. Suddenly I remembered what had happened to the tree that had flowed into me. It had been assimilated into me until nothing was left of it.

"What are you doing?" I barely managed to whisper.

"I'm sorry, Kiddo. But I have to do this."

*

There was only one person in the world who called me by that name.

"You're… Melissa."

I looked up at her, and she met my gaze with a smile and a nod.

"Took you a while to figure it out, Kiddo."

My mouth went dry. For a moment, I didn't care if I did die and

151

was assimilated into her. For a moment, I didn't feel the pain and weakness. For a moment, there was only one thing in the world that mattered.

"Why?" I croaked.

"Heaven's core code."

"That's all you wanted? The core code?"

"What did you think? That I really wanted you?"

My heart was stinging and screaming. Suddenly I wasn't Royal Black. Suddenly I was Roy Schwartz again, the same flaccid, ugly, disgusting high school student in love with a girl who mocked him. And deceived him. Again and again. I started crying. Why did she do this to me?

"All you had to do was ask," I whimpered.

I lay on the ground, my hands and legs held tight by the grass cuffs, my life force being sucked out of me into the woman that you could say I... I loved. Who, I had been certain, loved me. And now she looked at me with cold eyes. Possibly even angry eyes, I realized.

"When we were in the jungle, I asked you to run. Did you do it?"

I kept quiet.

She moved closer. Her face was no longer completely burnt, and her broken arm was healed. Her eyes got bigger. Her voice rose to a shout.

"And when I asked you what happened with the tree, did you tell me?"

Her eyes kept growing. They started to glow blue, like spotlights in the middle of her face. She was scary. Painfully beautiful, but scary.

"I didn't know," I stuttered. "I didn't know you were Melissa."

"You didn't know," she said with quiet contempt, and inhaled deeply twice. Finally, she sat down on the grass again, hugging her knees to her chest. The artery of life kept flowing from me into her at a steady pace. It wasn't a quick process. She had to wait for it to end.

"Don't take it personally, Kiddo. But even if you'd known who I was, there's no chance you'd have given me the core code. It's just not who you are."

She was right, of course.

"It was worth waiting thirty years to get to this moment."

*

152

-"Thirty years?"
-"Took the words right out of my mouth."

*

M looked at me, amused. "You really haven't figured it out yet?"
"What's to figure out?"
"You disappoint me. So smart... and so stupid."
She didn't say that to offend me, and I didn't take offense. It was just an accurate description of reality. She was up, I was down. She got it all and I, apparently, didn't understand anything. But she explained it to me.

"After you uploaded me to Heaven, you know what the first thing I did was? Made sure you wouldn't be uploaded. Or at least, that you wouldn't wake up immediately when you arrived, but only when I desired it."

"Trash you," I said, and closed my eyes.

I was tired, so tired. There was nothing I could do but surrender to the process and assimilate into her. I had lost. She had won. That was all that mattered at that moment, and even that wasn't important. At least she wasn't trying to hold me forever in some crystal prison of despair. Thirty years after my physical death, my real death would come. I kept sinking into blurred consciousness.

*

A squeaky, feline roar made me open my eyes. My vision was hazy. I heard the sounds of a struggle and then screams of pain. Different shadows came into my range of vision. I had to see what was going on! I made a great effort, blinked, and my focus returned.

On the grass, ten feet away from me, I saw a severed hand. It was covered in speckled fur.

A little beyond that was José Johnson, on his knees, writhing in pain. His left arm ended at the elbow and a jet of dark blood spewed out of it and stained the green grass. Over him loomed Melissa, all fire and rage, holding the purple fire sword. A deep laceration on her pale thigh exposed the bone, but I already knew the injury wouldn't really stop her. The cut was healing rapidly before my eyes, closing up, inch by inch. Across her abdomen and chest were ten deep, bleeding scratches shaped like a cat's claw. They, too, were healing.

Melissa seethed with anger. She lifted the sword over her head and was about to swing it down on José's neck.

But then a figure jumped her from behind. It, too, was speckled. And screaming in an inhuman voice.

Jackie! I wondered where she'd been hiding all this time.

With feline flexibility she coiled herself around Melissa's back, trying to forcefully hold on to her. Melissa tried to shake her off with a rapid spin, but Jackie held on. The spinning grew faster, turning into a blurry tornado. The artery of life that connected us was not damaged by it, just slowed down. But Jackie almost flew off due to the inertia.

At the last moment, she coiled her hand around Melissa's throat, extended her claws, and let go. The spinning did its job. She flew twenty feet away, rolled a few times on the ground, and looked back.

The artery in Melissa's neck had turned into a spinning sprinkler of blood. She collapsed to her knees, released the sword, and held on to her throat. Her entire body was painted in blood. I looked at the sight, mesmerized.

"Run! Run away!" I heard Jackie scream.

But I couldn't run away. I was trapped by the grass cuffs and couldn't free myself from them. To demonstrate how helpless I was, I tried lifting my right hand.

To my surprise, it actually rose.

"Don't move, Master," I heard a familiar voice say.

It was the leprechaun. He knelt by my side with a serrated knife in hand, sawing the stems holding my throat. "I'll get you out in a jiffy. Just don't move."

I turned my gaze back to Melissa. Jackie was already back on her, clawing her over and over again on the sides of her stomach. But that didn't seem to have any effect at all. Every time Jackie sunk her claws into Melissa's guts, they came out blood free. The cut on her neck was completely healed now. She wasn't reacting to the assault just yet, but I knew she would be completely recovered in a moment. My life force was helping her heal quickly. As long as our connection was active, Melissa would be untouchable.

My vision blurred again. "The artery!" I screeched as loudly as I could, grabbing the artery of life coming out of my heart. I shook it to illustrate. "Cut it…" I gasped.

Jackie looked at me and then at the beating artery. I saw understanding dawn in her eyes. She abandoned her attempts to stab

154

Melissa and pounced on the artery with claws extended. I tried to tell her to use the fire sword, but I could no longer speak. Jackie's claws couldn't penetrate the artery and the world slowly crumbled in front of my eyes.

In the meantime, Melissa had recuperated. She shook her head, looked around, and found the purple sword. With the sword now in her hand, she got to her feet and took a single step toward Jackie.

But then she stumbled and fell forward. Behind her, bleeding out of his stump, was José, holding on to her ankle with his remaining hand. His claws sunk into the pale foot and came out the other side, but that didn't do any damage. Melissa kicked him with her other foot. José flew up in the air and out of my range of sight. Melissa got back to her feet and started walking toward Jackie again. She twirled the sword in her hand like an expert.

Jackie was whimpering with anger. She tried to cut the cord with everything she had but with no success. She sunk her teeth into it, but the artery was still beating. Desperately she shook her head in all directions like a wild animal, the artery in her mouth, but that didn't work either.

Melissa appeared behind her: tall, angry, like a vindictive pale angel. She brought the sword up over her head and with a single sharp scream, swung it down forcefully.

*

Jackie's head rolled over the grass, landing next to me. Her eyes were still alive, looking around in panic. A jet of blood came out of her neck, staining me. Then her eyes faded and her head disappeared.

For a moment there was silence.

And then I heard a deep gurgling. I looked in the direction of the sound.

Melissa was lying alone on the grass. Her body was twitching, her face was distorted with pain. One end of the artery of life hung out of her stomach. It was stained with remnants of purple. The other end of the artery was writhing in the grass, cut clean by the fire sword.

"Are you ready, Master?" I heard Charlie say to my right.

All four cuffs were off. The artery was fading into the air. I was free. Melissa was still on the ground, her body twitching uncontrollably. It was my chance to get away from there. If only I

155

had the strength.

"Hold on," the leprechaun said, and started dragging me away. After a few seconds, he beamed toward the rainbow.

Taking me with him.

CONTACT

I let myself rest.

It was the only thing I could have done. I was on the brink of death, there was nothing I could do anyway. Melissa had cut the cord just a moment before everything I had flowed into her. But not a whole lot was left now. A little bit of me and a little bit of Heaven's core code. I could barely speak, barely move. I let Charlie take me where he wanted, do with me what he thought was right.

Our first stop was the rainbow pool. He got there after a few hundred beams, a lot more than I would have needed. But he was just an AI, and he had to carry me with him.

The last few beams were inside the jungle, and I noticed it had turned scary again. I smiled to myself. Charlie was cleverly trying to prevent Melissa from chasing him.

As for me, I was terrified. The trees were evil, the scent of death was in the air, and at any given moment, a hideous monster was going to attack and eat me. If I'd had the strength, I'd have run away. But I didn't. And for that, I was blessed.

We arrived at the pool. Charlie placed me gently into it, and then came in after me.

The feel of the color water worked wonders. It calmed, it healed, and it strengthened. I floated in it with my eyes closed and limbs relaxed, letting its power seep into me. I was slowly able to move again. Wiggle my fingers, clench my fists, move my hands and legs. I was still very weak, but Charlie was patient and held on to me tightly.

Eventually, I could let go of him and float in the water by myself. I couldn't beam yet.

It was a slow process, and time was not on my side. I knew Melissa wouldn't leave me alone. As long as I had part of the core code, she'd come after me, find me, and suck everything out of me. The leprechaun's barrier of fear wouldn't hold her back for long. And what could I do? Most of the core code was in her hands. Once she found a way to control it, she could change Heaven effortlessly. If there was a God in Heaven, she was the one that was going to be the closest thing to it.

To keep on surviving, I needed help. But I had no one to ask for it. Rage and his gang had been dispersed and neutralized and wouldn't have helped me anyway. I was new to Heaven and still didn't have any friends. José and Jackie were most likely in an awakening room now. At best. I hoped Melissa wouldn't go after them. But I imagined it was only a matter of time. She had waited thirty years to deal with me. She wouldn't forget them either. They would become hunted. No one would want any involvement with them. Or with me.

The last option was to locate the Resistance members - the Newborn who had infiltrated Heaven, whom Rage had locked up. There might be hundreds of them, but maybe far fewer. After all, Rage had locked up some people who had nothing to do with the Resistance. But still, surely some of them belonged to the Newborn - and now they were free. Almost certainly, the woman with the flag tattoo was one of them. The monk in the orange robe as well, the one who had interrogated me outside of Midlake. But I had no idea how to find them. A dead end.

A dead end.

I had to think outside the box. Outside the system. Outside the -

And suddenly I knew.

"The Plain of Souls," I said to Charlie. "Take me to the Plain of Souls."

"Yes, Master. Hold on."

＊

It was a long and boring road. But at its end, I stood in the middle of the plain, dark and angry skies above me, one of the wells at my feet. I tried to make it work. To make it open up for me. This time, unlike my previous visit, I knew what I wanted and for whom I was aiming. But the well did not respond. Either I was too weak, or something inside me just made it difficult to communicate this way. I tried once, twice, ten times. The well did not respond.

I kicked one of the stones around the well. The silence around was irritating and difficult, as always. I imagined it must be temporary. Soon, Melissa would track me down and then the pixies would arrive, or thunder rats, or other creatures. My time here was very limited.

"I can't establish a connection," I said to Charlie.

"Yes, Master. I see that."

"I have to establish a connection."

"If you say so, Master."

"Maybe I can ask someone to make contact for me? What do you think?"

The leprechaun looked around. "You can try, Master. But there is no one around."

I looked at him in despair. He smiled at me and flipped a gold coin in the air. The coin flipped a few times and fell back to his hand. It disappeared and in its place appeared a pipe. He puffed on it and a few smoke rings floated up and created a crown over his head.

"I wish you could make the well work," I sighed.

Charlie pulled the pipe out of his mouth and stuffed additional tobacco in it. "But I can, Master," he said.

"What? You can make the well work?"

"Of course."

"What? So why didn't you say that earlier?"

"Because you didn't ask, Master."

I kicked the stone again. "Idiot, idiot, idiot. Okay, connect me please. You know who Jerri.Co is?"

The leprechaun smiled.

*

"Who are you again?"

It was hard for me to answer. From the well, a sixty-year-old man spoke to me. What was left of his gray hair barely covered his head. There were dark circles under his eyes. He wore a checkered work shirt and an old pair of jeans that had been fixed a few times, badly. He spoke to me from within a dismal, rustic greenhouse made out of wood boards. The greenhouse was full of oxygen algae.

I barely recognized him. Still, for him it had been thirty years, even if for me we had spoken barely a month ago.

"I am Roy Schwartz."

Jerri.Co stayed silent for a few seconds. I could almost sense the wheels turning.

"You don't look like Roy Schwartz," he finally answered, but did not turn off the holo.

"You don't look like yourself, either."

"It's called aging," he sighed. "I'm going to ask one last time: who are you?"

159

"Roy Schwartz," I repeated. "I succeeded in uploading to Heaven."

His eyes scanned me and I knew what he was thinking. He always looked for the stinger. The catch. Like every old hacker, Jerri.Co was aware of the fact he was always at war. Under surveillance. They were always trying to get him, and he always had to be on guard. I smiled to myself. He must be trying to understand what would make someone bring up a ghost from his past and challenge him that way.

"Well, good for you," he finally said. "So you're Roy Schwartz. What's that got to do with me?"

"I know you don't believe me," I said, and heard him agree with a snort of contempt. "But what I'm asking is for you to try for a moment. To pretend for a moment that you succeeded."

He hesitated for a second.

"That I succeeded in what?"

"That you succeeded in uploading me to Heaven. Thirty years ago."

He laughed without smiling. "I don't know what you want, but I suggest you stop. I've suffered enough from the likes of you."

I furrowed my brows. This conversation was taking an unexpected turn. I hate unexpected turns. "What exactly do you mean?"

"Oh, stop it! Isn't it enough you all but ruined my life? You got what you wanted! I didn't go online for thirty years, I get no renewed body treatments, and I'm stuck in this air farm with this trashing algae! Why do you keep coming back to me? Let me die in peace."

Now he was on the verge of crying.

I considered hanging up the call. Let him be. I understood he couldn't help me anymore if he'd had no access to the grid for thirty years.

"I'm sorry to have bothered you," I said finally. "Have a nice day."

"Yeah, yeah." He lifted an angry gaze to me. "Have a trash day -"

And then his pupils widened a little. He didn't look straight into my eyes, but a little to the side, beyond my shoulder.

"What? Who is that?" he asked, suspicious.

I looked round as well. There was no one there but Charlie, who was busy bouncing eight gold coins in his hand in an elaborate routine. Without stopping the motion, the leprechaun came close and peeked into the well, curious. And then he waved and waved hello with his free hand.

"Hey, Jerry!" The leprechaun bounced a gold coin in his hand.

"Do you know Master named me? You can call me Charlie now!"

Jerri.Co looked back at me slowly with a surprised look.

"Roy?"

And then he wept, his body wracked with sobs.

*

-*"So what really happened to him?"*

-*"He said they caught him after they broke into my house. They followed the brain link."*

-*"So, how is he even alive? Or conscious? Why didn't he get erased?"*

-*"He said he cut a deal with them. To keep living, he took down his whole net and a few other hackers' nets. In addition, they blocked him out of the grid and took away his option to change organs."*

-*"That's a death sentence. Slow and ugly."*

*

After thirty years, Jerri.Co was perhaps older and slower, but just as clever. Just as rebellious. He hated the system just as much. And, apparently, he had safeguarded a few surprises, the most important of which was the backup of the material I had given him before I uploaded into Heaven. It wasn't the consciousness backup. Just a part of the special powers I had developed. And most importantly, a few algorithms for error detection and correction.

If I could only put my hands on those pieces of code, I could fix myself. Or at least challenge Melissa. I looked at Charlie, full of hope. As always, he didn't really pay attention to me. Only to his gold coins, which he continued to bounce perfectly.

"But I can't send it directly to you," Jerri.Co said from within the well.

"I know, I know, you're not connected. It's okay. I need you to get to Boulder, Colorado. Inside the system complex -"

He interjected mid-sentence, shaking his head with a sad no.

"Why not? What happened?" I asked.

"I can't go there. It's a war zone now."

I swallowed hard. "What war? I thought -"

The next instant, the air around me was filled with the loud noise of giant, buzzing wings. A gust of wind slammed me down on the ground and two dragonflies landed in front of me. Another dragonfly

161

appeared right above me and three more behind me and to my sides.

Even Charlie didn't get a chance to run away. An orange acid jet caught him where he sat, and he melted in it.

Eight gold coins landed on the dusty ground.

VISIT

A few seconds later, Melissa beamed in front of me.

Something in her color had changed. Instead of the white marble shade, she was glowing from within. Just like a lamp. Against the white light coming from her, her mouth was as cherry red as ever, and her blue eyes twinkled. This time, the pasties were shaped like stars, and in her right hand she held a whip. It was made out of shining white light.

When she smiled, she was beautiful. When she didn't smile, she was divine.

"Did you really think you could run away from me, Roy?"

I glanced at the well. It was dark. I didn't know who had shut it off, but I hoped Melissa hadn't noticed Jerri.Co and that he was protected from her. But then I realized something: Who cared if she saw him? Jerri.Co lived in another world, a different universe almost. Melissa had no way of harming him. If anything, the opposite was true. I smiled, relieved.

"Why would I want to run away from you, Melissa?"

She didn't like my answer. Her whip moved slowly and its tip made little circles in the air. I imagined how it would feel on my skin when she decided to use it. She began circling me slowly, eyeing me as if we were in a Byzantine slave market. I remained where I was, motionless. I didn't follow her with my eyes. I just stood there.

Her circle brought her to the space between me and the darkened well. She snuck a look in it, then came back and looked at me curiously. The desire to meet her eyes was powerful, but I made an effort and kept looking at a distant point on the horizon. I tried beaming to it, but the only result was a wave of pain splitting my head.

She kept circling me and eventually stopped behind me. Very close. Too close.

"What are you doing here?" she whispered.

Her voice was sweet. The scent coming off her was intoxicating. I struggled not to respond.

"I came to watch the news."

I closed my eyes and gritted my teeth. I expected a lash on my back. But it didn't come. Instead, she decided to abuse me in more effective ways.

She exhaled over the back of my neck. I trembled.

"And... was it good... the news?"

My heart was racing wildly. I hated myself. I tried to escape her, get away from her, detach myself from her, but before I even took a single step, her hand touched me from behind. I froze in place.

"It's never good, the news," I managed to mumble.

She let go of me.

"Sit."

Out of thin air, a small, comfortable-looking woven chair appeared. Melissa laid her hand on my shoulder and gently guided me into it. After that, as if in slow motion, she fell back, and at the last second before she hit the ground, a comfortable sofa appeared under her, breaking her fall.

She crossed her legs in front of me. The whip lightly rested next to her naked knee.

"The really bad news, Roy – Royal - is, in fact, the real reason I woke you up."

She paused, as if she was expecting me to ask her about it. But I didn't want to give her that satisfaction. If she had something to tell me, she could just tell me. If there wasn't anything she wanted to tell me, I wasn't going to make her life easier. We stayed silent together for a few seconds and eventually she continued.

"What do you know about the Newborn?"

"Rage asked me the same thing. What am I supposed to know about them?"

"Don't play with me, Trash."

"I don't want to play with you. Can I go now?"

I got up off the chair. I mean I tried to. It didn't work.

"They're terrorists," Melissa continued, ignoring my attempt to end the conversation. "They're mostly old school Evangelical Christians, but not exclusively. Some are just ordinary people who can't get into Heaven simply because they have no money."

This time, I did react. "Rightly so. Heaven should be open to everyone."

"Maybe it should, maybe it shouldn't. That's surely a subject for discussion. The problem is that neither you nor I determine who'll get in here. As you know, they didn't let me in either -"

"Until I got you in!"

"Until you got me in. And thank you for that, by the way. But that's not the point. We're talking about the Newborn and the fact that all they're interested in is destroying Heaven."

Up to that moment, she hadn't said anything new. But I didn't stop her. As long as she was talking, I was in good shape. Then I wondered to myself why she was still talking to me. I was expecting to be on the ground by now, with the cord pulling what was left of me into her. Why hadn't it happened yet?

"So, about the Newborn," I answered. "Rage said some of them were in the crystal prison."

"That's true. Some of them uploaded into Heaven just to try and destroy it from within."

"Why would they do that?"

She shrugged. "How should I know? They say it's blasphemy. That it spits in the face of God. Stealing souls."

"But why do they care?" I protested.

For a moment, I forgot what Melissa had done to me. For a moment, we were on the same side again. The side that wanted to live.

"You can't really understand fanatics. They want to either turn you into one of them or destroy you. Like the Caliphate, that wants to make the whole world Muslim. The Newborn aren't much different."

She lifted her legs up onto the sofa and stretched out. The atmosphere was much more relaxed, and I felt she was enjoying talking to me. I looked into her eyes with something close to naughtiness, trying to fan that flame.

"A lot has changed in the world in thirty years."

"Yes… and it's only the beginning. The beginning of the end."

"Explain."

She smiled. "Do you think life downstairs is going to get better? That the air will be healthier to breathe? You were the one watching the news earlier. Did they say how many billions have died from violence in the last decade?"

I knew how many billions had died. But I still didn't understand what it had to do with me. I let her go on.

"The world downstairs is on the brink of mass obliteration. It happens once every ten million years."

I knew what mass obliteration was. "But that's not what's happening now, Melissa. We are in control."

She shook her head no.

165

"We're not in control at all. In the last hundred years, over ninety-five percent of the species on Earth became instinct. Oxygen levels are dropping. The weather's changing. Africa is a disaster area. And now with the Caliphate… it's only a matter of time until war breaks out. The war."

I kept quiet.

"The last place that will remain civilized will be Heaven. Rage understood that. The whole system understood that," she continued. "That's why they're gathering all human knowledge here. This is humanity's lifeboat."

I could agree with that. But there was one thing I didn't understand.

"Then why are you opposing them?"

"Because they're doing it wrong!" she shouted. "They can't keep Heaven safe. The Newborn will win and Heaven will be destroyed."

I leaned back. I still needed to know more. I had to taunt her.

"I don't think that will happen," I said stubbornly.

"Idiot trash kid! Because of them, Heaven is being destroyed. Right at this moment! Here, look."

She flicked her whip once in the air and the well came to life. It was not the holo, but a flat picture coming from the security cameras of the system's underground complex. The broadcast jumped from one camera to the other, trying to capture everything.

The corridors were filled with smoke. In one of them I saw a number of dead bodies. Some of them wore the stars and stripes of the Newborn. Other bodies were security guards in black armored suits. There were bodies of regular staff members in civilian clothes. Melissa flicked again. The picture switched to another corridor filled with smashed computers parts and furniture. Another lash of the whip and the picture switched to a different corridor full of smoke, where there was some human movement. A bunch of people were shooting at some target out of camera range. One after the other, they were shot down and fell to the floor. A Newborn squadron rushed into frame and kept charging onward.

"They didn't guard the complex well enough," she said in her mind. "They underestimated the Newborn's sophistication. I tried to warn them! But Rage wouldn't listen. That's why I woke you up."

"To take down Rage for you?"

She hesitated for a moment. Starting to speak, then stopping, then continuing again.

"No. I could have taken Rage down on my own, in time. He's not as strong as he looks, and I had friends."

"So?"

She inhaled deeply. "I woke you up for a different reason. Here, look."

Melissa kept whipping. The images coming from the well changed rapidly. She found what she was looking for after seven tries. It was one of the Newborn, a large man, dragging a hoverplate with a large suitcase on it. He moved down an utterly wrecked corridor. A quiet corridor, which had already seen a battle. Suddenly he stopped and another man came into the frame, wearing the stars and stripes, armed with a heavy rifle. They exchanged words and the young man tried to take the hoverplate from the older man. In response, the older man slapped him across the face and yelled a few mute commands.

The young man stood to attention, eyes lowered. After a few seconds, the older man softened and patted his shoulder, pointing to the hallway in front of them. The young man saluted and ran back where he had come from. The older man continued in the same direction, dragging the suitcase behind him.

"That's their commander," she said after the hallway was empty. "He's carrying a gamma bomb."

That was weird to watch.

Technically, those halls were right next to me. Around me, you could say. Practically, they were in another galaxy. We were at the heart of a barren desert, under an apocalyptic afternoon sky, black and red, with lightning and thunder echoing in the background. Beyond that, with one breath we could be next to the raging color waterfall spilling into a rainbow pool, under the bluest sky ever seen, and breathing sweet, scented air. We could also be at the top of a snow-covered mountain, breathing the clean, crisp fragrance. We could surf the kind of wave that had never existed on Earth.

And we could share a bed. And a life. Just the two of us, a black Adam and a white Eve. In complete serenity.

Still, in that serenity, there was a crowded and heated war zone. And ghosts of soldiers killing each other somewhere among the wrecked corridors, under a deep mountain, on a planet we once lived and died on.

We shouldn't have been a part of that battle. Yet we were.

"That bomb is going to destroy the whole complex," Melissa went

167

on, "and when it does, Heaven will disappear. We will all die. For good."

"I've been dead for thirty years," I said dryly.

I didn't care. Why would I? Melissa was going to destroy me anyway. To assimilate me into her or, in the worst case, keep me in another crystal prison. I'd no doubt she had the ability. And I couldn't fight anymore. I remembered Rage's last words before she had buried him in the ground. "You're making a mistake," he had said.

And right he was. Most of the core code was in her. I had no more tricks up my sleeve.

So I was ready to let Heaven be destroyed. Actually, the more I thought about it, the happier I was. If I was going to go, then I wanted to go like that. In fireworks. If I could, I would sing happily and mock her all the way to hell, while she watched the holo, the Newborn forces continued to take over more and more of the complex, on their way to blowing it all up. I don't think I could have gotten better revenge.

Melissa gritted her teeth angrily. I could see her jaw muscles clench and her fists curl. I waited for her response. I knew it would be painful. I just didn't know how much.

"I know where your mother is."

*

-"Trash!"
-"Trash."

*

My heart skipped a beat.

"After you uploaded her to Heaven, I picked her packet up and kept it."

The thought hit me like a punch in the gut. Adrenaline kick started my body again. Even in the midst of the great despair that consumed me, for a moment I felt hope. Purpose. I tried to get up, excited. I couldn't get up off the chair, of course. "Where is she?" I yelled.

Melissa kept talking in the same monotone voice. "I kept her, for a moment like this."

168

"Where is she?" I whispered. I knew the answer would come with a heavy price.

"Somewhere safe." She smiled. "I can wake her up whenever I want. Of course, if there's nowhere to wake up to..."

She let that sentence die slowly, along with my hope.

"You WILL go downstairs. And you WILL stop him."

I rolled my eyes in frustration. "What makes you think I, of all people, can stop him? I'm the last one who can do it!"

Her eyes raked over me hungrily.

"On the contrary, Royal," she said. "You are the only one who can do it."

*

I sat down in the chair again. I leaned back. If things had been a little different, I would have smiled. Because those were the words I wanted to hear. When you're the only one that can deliver the goods, you're the one who sets the price. But things were not different. So I didn't smile. My price wasn't high, either.

"I'm willing to do it on one condition," I said.

She crossed her delicate arms across her chest.

"Yes?"

"I want to say good-bye to my mother."

"That's not going to happen."

"I'm serious. I want to see her first."

"I can't wake her up now. It's a process that takes time."

I inhaled deeply. I knew, of course, from experience, that it was a process that takes time. But I also knew that it just has to get started. And that doesn't take time. I couldn't trust Melissa to act on it after I gave her what she wanted. She just wouldn't see the need to make the effort. She'd forget about the whole thing.

But if I could get her to start the process before I headed on my way, I would give Mom a real chance. In that case, Melissa would have to make an effort in order to stop the process. And why would she do that? She'd just forget about the whole thing. And I was counting on that.

"I don't care. I want to see her in the awakening room. Without that, I'm not moving."

Melissa shook all over. For a moment I thought she would just strangle me right there. Or finally use her threatening whip. How

169

long could she wait, after all?

But she took a deep breath and peeked into the well. Inside it, the security camera showed the fat man continuing to drag the hovering suitcase down the hall. The bomb kept ticking.

Melissa clapped.

DEPORTATION

A giant dragonfly appeared above me.

With finesse and accuracy, it opened its mouth, grabbed me, and closed its jaws around me. I tried to be careful not to get cut, but that wasn't really under my control. The dragonfly could cut me in half at any given moment. Melissa, for her part, climbed onto it easily and relaxed on its back. I could see one of her feet hanging off each side.

We took off.

The wind whistled in my ears. It was loud, but not loud enough to prevent us from talking. Beyond that, it was Heaven. You don't really have to speak to someone to talk to them.

"What are you going to do with me later?" I asked.

"There will be no later."

"Are you going to kill me?"

"Like you said: you've been dead for thirty years, Kiddo."

That was the price, apparently. For the remainder of the flight I kept quiet.

It was more comfortable than I expected. Much faster too. Dragonflies, it turns out, can beam across very long distances. In three minutes we were at El-Paso, above the forest. In a few seconds, we landed. Its jaws opened and I was free.

From a distance, I could see people moving away quickly, beaming out of the forest in all directions, panicked. In Heaven, no one wanted to be near a dragonfly.

Melissa clapped her hands.

*

I found myself in one of the awakening rooms. Everything was white. Everything was shining. I had visited here twice and both times were accompanied by extreme pain. This time it wasn't.

Not physical pain, that is.

In the corner of the room, over a white bed, a glowing figure was forming. Its body didn't exist yet. Instead, there were white and gold sparks, like little fireflies bouncing around. Near where a head should be, the sparks were closer together. Slowly I started seeing the eyes.

171

They were squinting in pain. A familiar mouth, loved, was open in a silent cry.

Melissa was standing behind me. "Come on. Say good-bye. And fast."

I had trouble finding the words. I remembered how hard it was for me, when I had just uploaded to Heaven. I hoped Mother could cope with that pain better than I could. Maybe she really could. Maybe it was easier for women. After all, they experience birth, while we pop zits, at most. Mother's face came together, and the expression on it grew more and more tormented. I hoped she could hear me. I prayed that if she really could, maybe she would understand me, too.

"Mom," I whispered, coming closer. "I kept my promise. I brought you here."

Slowly I kissed what would be her forehead. It tingled.

"Roy?" she whispered.

"Mom? I'm here."

She wasn't breathing. She didn't need to breathe, so at first she just made shapes with her lips without air coming through them. After a few seconds she breathed again consciously, and that was how she could keep talking.

"Did we make it?"

A warm tear fell from my eye onto her chin. "Yes, Mom, we made it."

She opened her eyes. "You look… different."

"I know. You'll look different, too. Now rest."

"Will you be here when I wake up?"

I took a deep breath.

"Yes, Mom. I'll wait for you."

Her expression calmed. My answer satisfied her. I tried to imagine what she was thinking about. I knew she was in pain, but unlike me, she had all her memories. For her, it hadn't been thirty years. From her perspective, it was only a fraction of a second after she fell asleep on my bed. In our home. And now she expected to see Heaven from the inside, with me.

"Good. You're a good boy, Roy."

She closed her eyes and blacked out.

I took a step back. I couldn't see anything through the screen of tears that clouded my vision. I couldn't even say a single word. I wished, in my heart, that she would succeed in forgetting these moments. That she would understand and forgive me one day.

Melissa clapped her hands.

*

We were back at the Plain of Souls.

It was deserted and gloomier than ever. A strong wind swept grains of sand into the air. They got in my eyes, making me blink.

"Come on." Melissa went back to commanding. "He's already making the bomb."

I nodded and stepped forward. I bent over and looked inside the well.

It, of course, did not illuminate.

"I don't even know how to get to him." I looked at Melissa helplessly. "How do you expect me to -"

With a swift, impatient move, she came to stand beside me and then looked down into the well.

This time it illuminated instantly.

The corridor where the camera was located was completely destroyed. The walls were charred and pierced from gun shots. The floor was filled with holes and chunks of the wall that had crashed down. The camera moved to the right, and in the distance I could see people moving quickly. Shots flashed into my vision. People screamed and fell down without a sound. In the back, a soldier wearing stars and stripes jumped into my line of sight. A security guard dressed in black was chasing him. Both were trying to shoot each other and both missed, point blank. The Newborn lunged first and grabbed the security guard's throat.

The guard fought back wildly. Without meaning to, one of his knees hit the Newborn between his legs and made him collapse. A second kick, well-aimed this time, broke his nose. The security guard started kicking the Newborn's head again and again. Even after the Newborn stopped moving, he was still going.

Then three shots pierced the guard's chest, and he crumpled.

One of the closets moved. From behind it came the fat man I'd seen earlier. The commander. He wasn't stable. In his right hand he held a gun, but he held his left hand against his chest. His shirt was torn, and under it was, I assumed, a bulletproof vest. With every breath, his face twitched in pain.

Behind him floated the suitcase with the gamma bomb. He checked it for a moment and then looked straight at the camera.

173

Right at me. For a moment he pointed the gun straight at my eyes.

"Stop!" I yelled.

The man didn't respond.

"He can't hear or see you," Melissa said behind me. "This is a one-way communication."

If so, then he just wanted to shoot the security camera. But after another second, he smiled and lowered his gun. His eyes darted from side to side, looking for more targets. Fresh blood was smeared on his forehead, over his eyes. He cast a last look at the camera and then spit on the floor with contempt.

"Recognize him?" Melissa asked me.

For some reason, he looked familiar. But not familiar enough.

"That's their commander, isn't it?"

"You're such an idiot sometimes," she said to herself.

And then she told me who you are.

*

-*"Trash."*

-*"I'm proud to say, it only took me a few seconds for the information to sink in. Somehow it even made sense. And explained a lot of things. I almost laughed."*

*

I looked at Melissa one last time, trying to find some sign of tenderness. Some compassion. If she had either of those, she hid them well. Then she pointed her finger at the well.

I didn't get it.

"You said earlier that it's a one-way communication. He can't hear me."

"Not through the screen. But you're about to really talk to him. Face-to-face."

"How's that possible? I'm dead. We're up here."

"I want you to go downstairs."

I wrinkled my forehead, puzzled. Go downstairs? I looked at the well again. It was very deep. I remembered the first time I came here I had wondered how deep it was. And what was on the other side of it.

"This well is connected to the first Heaven prototype," she

174

explained. "It's long been out of active use, but I managed to activate it. It will contain your mind. And it has a screen."

I looked down at the well. Finally, I knew what was waiting on the other side. I wondered if anyone had ever tried to climb into it.

"And after I go down?"

She lifted her hands to the sides and shook her head a little. She expressed no joy, but she didn't express any great sorrow. I understood the rest on my own.

"You're going to unplug me from Heaven."

"Yes."

It was all up to me, it turned out. Everything. My life. Her life. The life of everyone in Heaven. Everyone I had met along the way and would maybe meet someday, if Melissa let me live. But above all, one thing mattered the most.

"You'll let Mom live, right?"

Melissa nodded her head.

"Yes, I will let her live, I promise. She's done nothing wrong."

"Neither did I."

"That's true, Royal. Roy. But you're different. You're just… a threat."

I inhaled deeply, then exhaled. What possible threat was I to her?

"You don't know why?" She answered my thoughts. For a moment I thought she was sad. "You're just too dangerous. You know Heaven too well. You know me too well. I'd prefer it if you were not so dangerous. You're a good time."

"How can I be sure you'll take care of my mother?"

She shrugged. "You can't. You'll have to trust me. But if you don't hurry," she nodded toward the well, "I can guarantee only one thing: your mother will never wake up here."

*

I had no choice. Maybe I could try to fight her. I'd probably last a little while. Perhaps I'd even win. But… but then I wouldn't have had any time to talk to you. And I had to do it. Otherwise, you'd have activated this bomb next to you and me… and Mother…

So I went into the well and started climbing down. On hand after the other, one leg after the other.

All along, I kept looking up at her blue eyes, glowing in the most beautiful face I had ever seen. Behind her floated red and gray clouds,

175

shooting out mute lightning under an eternal dusk. I was banned from Heaven and my heart pinched.

The descent took a little over a minute. At some point, I stopped looking at Melissa, and when I looked back up again the well had turned off and everything was dark. Eventually I lost my grip and fell. When I got up, I found myself here. It's a very small room with a little screen. I don't even know where I am, physically. Probably in one of the corners of this complex. But it doesn't matter, because the system is the same system. When you push the button and blow this place to smithereens, I'll be gone with it.

It's funny. Because now that I know you, of all people, are trying to ruin Heaven, I kind of understand why. And I even feel a little proud, that out of everyone, you have succeeded. No one else was smart enough to pull it off.

But now you also know who I am.

The power is in your hands, man. All I can do is ask. Plead. Don't kill me.

Don't kill yourself. And most importantly: don't kill Mother.

DECISION

The holo before me flickered and powered off.

I was having trouble breathing, partly because of the harsh smell of charred circuits, but also because of the bullets that had hit my chest earlier. My lack of fitness didn't help. I sat down heavily on one of the few chairs that had remained intact. I used the minutes I had left to rest and process what the muscular black man with the blue eyes had told me over the past few hours.

It was quite a lot. He had talked and talked, only occasionally pausing to answer my questions. Through the holo I could feel his fatigue, his desperation. But he was me, so many years ago. And I was still a little him. A little childish. Thirty years ago, when I was his age, when I was him, I would probably have done the same thing. Give the speech, feel just, and then fall silent. I knew that kid well.

And I remembered, vaguely, what he was talking about.

I suddenly remembered things I hadn't remembered in years. Things they had erased from me. But now, when he talked about them, I knew they were true. They had really happened. I remembered, very vaguely, the entrance to Heaven and the tours I took in it. LOOM! I haven't played that in years... I don't even know if the game still exists. But I do know I enjoyed playing it.

I tried to guess what the pale woman he spoke of looked like. Melissa. I could remember her, barely. Her weird visit, a million-year-old woman inside the body of a forty-year-old. I remembered what she had done to me. What I did to her. What I did to dispose of her body.

I tried to ask Black one more thing, but his holo had shut off.

I was left alone in the last hallway of the complex. Of the group that was with me, only I had survived. And it was alright, just fine. All the Newborn volunteered to die for the truth, and only one of us was needed to do what needed to be done.

I leaned against the wall, pondering what he had said to me. All those years I had worked to erase Heaven from the face of the Earth, without even visiting there once, without exposing myself to the abomination. And now, I remembered I had been there. I had been there a lot. Thirty years ago. So much time had passed.... And the last month before they arrested me... suddenly I remembered it existed. That I was alive through it, and I had done things in it I remembered.

I stood there for almost ten minutes without the ability to move, alone in the hallway. The bomb was next to me, waiting to be activated. But I couldn't. I had to let everything he said sink in. To remember what he was remembering.

I didn't remember the moment I committed suicide, but I did remember the moment I woke up. It wasn't as painful as when he woke up. And the room was not white at all. And instead of a sexy, addictive beauty, two old doctors and a policeman stood next to me. They had succeeded in rescuing me at the last moment, the shitheads. Who asked them to, anyway?

And then there was the trial, then the memory erasing, then prison.

I cringed when I remembered the prison. There, I hadn't been a muscular black man, but a fat, scared boy, the ass everyone wanted to get. I remembered the beatings, the showers, the tears, and the pain. Until one man had stepped forward and said, "No more." He defended me. He showed me the light. He put me in a real place, in the real life. It didn't matter to me that he was Christian and I wasn't. It was just important for him to show me the truth and help me understand that this world that I had wanted to get into so badly when they came to arrest me was just a big virtual lie. Heaven could not be Heaven. No man or computer system could play God.

But maybe it could?

Because Royal Black was me. And maybe he was a better version of me. After all, he hadn't taken out 3000 men in the past week just to get in here. He just wanted to save Mom.

Mom, whom I had killed thirty years ago. Mom, whose grave I went to every year in devotion. In great respect.

But she wasn't really dead. She could be resurrected, live again. Inside Heaven. But was that really coming back to life? Was that how life should be?

I moved closer to the bomb and looked at it.

I knew exactly what I had to do.

FROM THE AUTHOR

On August 18th, 2013, my father passed away.

A week earlier, in the morning, we had a merry family dinner. He was staying at our house after many years of living abroad. He played with his grandchildren, had fun with the cats, and went to the living room to rest on the couch.

After an hour, in his sleep, he had a stroke. A blood clot traveled from the side of one of his arteries, swept away by the blood stream. It clogged the artery bringing blood to the left side of his brain. The result: full paralysis of the right side of his body, loss of consciousness, and a week later, death.

He was sixty-six years old, young in today's terms.

My father died and I had a pain-filled hole in my heart and life. And inside this hole, thoughts sprouted. Why did he have to die? Why do we all have to die? I don't want to die. Not just for me. But for my children too. I want to live forever, for them. To continue and protect them, continue keeping them safe. I wish there was a way for that to happen. But there isn't. Yet.

On August 18th, 2013, my father passed away.

And this book was born.

ABOUT THE AUTHOR

L. L. Fine lives in a small town in Israel, and is taught humility and manners by his three charming children, loving wife, demanding cats, noisy neighbors and awesome readers.

Printed in Great Britain
by Amazon.co.uk, Ltd.,
Marston Gate.